A FOREVER KIND
OF LOVE

KRISTA LAKES

ZIRCONIA PUBLISHING, INC.

ABOUT THIS BOOK

"I've wanted this all my life," he said. "I want you."

Carter

Between running a company and a recent attempt on his life, billionaire Carter Williamson doesn't need any more stress. So when a trio of orphan children breaks into the Colorado ranch he's hiding out in, his first instinct is to just let the police handle it. That was before their spunky social worker Mia showed up.

Mia

Mia Amesworth has worked hard to make sure that the Smith kids aren't separated from each other, but she can only do so much. With her own body unable to produce children, the kids are the closest thing to a family she's got. When the handsome ranch owner offers to let the three troublemakers pay for the damages with hard work over the summer, she happily accepts. When he suggests they go on a date, she can't say yes fast enough.

Even though Carter's secret assailant keeps threatening him, he feels like he might be falling for the small town girl. And though Mia knows that a family might not be in the cards for her future, she longs to create a life with Carter.

And then, a miracle happens...

~

He smiled, then pulled back a little bit. "I do have one last surprise for you this evening," he said.

He turned and put his hand back in his pocket as if he was going to make a phone call. Mia grabbed his tie and pulled him back in for another kiss, and he pulled his hand out of his pocket. "It'll have to wait," she whispered into his ear.

"Yes, ma'am," he said with a smile. She put her hand on his chest and kissed again, feeling his heart rate increase as she became more assertive. This time, she leaned toward him, and as she moved her hands to his sides, she made sure to catch his suit coat and move it off his shoulders, letting it fall to the floor.

Carter's hands moved to the bottom of his shirt, where he began to undo his buttons, all while still kissing Mia. When he got to the top of his shirt, he began to loosen his tie. Again, Mia grabbed his tie and stopped him. "Keep it on," she said, surprised at her own tone.

He grinned from ear to ear and popped his collar, slipping the tie from the shirt to his skin. Then he took a step back, throwing the shirt off in a dramatic motion. For a moment, Mia marveled at the hard body in front of her. This was clearly a guy who not only rode horses but also spent a ton of time at the gym.

"Wow." Her mouth watered at the sight of him.

He smiled. Then stepped forward and his hand touched the fabric of her dress, sending shivers through her. "You know, when I saw this dress, all I could think about was how good you'd look in it." Mia smiled and blushed a little bit. He continued talking. "But now, I'm afraid the only thing I can think about is how good you'll look out of it."

Mia couldn't help but giggle a little bit. She reached back to unclasp the back, but in a moment his hands were around her, reaching up her back. "Please, allow me," he said as if he were the perfect gentleman for offering to disrobe her. She felt him deftly release the clasp, as sure of himself as when he uncorked the champagne. He moved the zipper down slowly, agonizingly slowly.

As soon as the zipper was at the bottom of her back, he leaned down and moved his lips to her neck, kissing down to her shoulder. She could feel his stubble against her skin, and it felt incredible. His hands moved to her shoulders, gently moving the straps of the dress.

With a whisper, the dress fell to the floor, leaving her in nothing but her panties. For a moment, she thought about covering herself, but she stopped herself. She knew this was coming and had never felt so comfortable in front of a man. She wanted to be seen by him...

For my boys

Chapter 1

$\mathcal{M}$ia

"ARE you the parent or legal guardian of Grayson and Alexander Smith?"

The cold voice on the other end of the phone made Mia's heart drop.

"I'm their social worker, Mia Amesworth," she replied, slowly stopping as she walked through the outdoor parking lot of the grocery store. "Are they okay?"

"The boys broke into Stone Mountain Ranch, ma'am." The voice was authoritative and uncompromising.

"Grayson and Alexander did what?" Mia came to an immediate and abrupt halt. It was a good thing no one else was leaving the building yet, or she probably would have been hit by a car since she was standing in the middle of the road.

"They broke into Stone Mountain Ranch, ma'am," the

voice repeated. "The boys said the person to contact about this was you."

"Have the police been contacted?" Mia asked as she started walking as quickly as possible toward her car. If she sped, she might be able to make it to the ranch before the police took the boys into custody. She thought about dropping her groceries and just running to the car.

"No ma'am," the male voice replied. "We wanted to inform you first."

Mia threw her groceries into the trunk without looking and slammed the door shut. "I'll be there in five minutes," she promised. "If you could wait to contact the police until I get there, I would appreciate it."

"Five minutes," the voice repeated and then hung up.

Mia cursed and sent a plea out into the universe that there wouldn't be any speed traps on the ten-minute drive to the ranch. She was afraid the universe might put all red stoplights on her route just to spite the boys. It seemed like the universe didn't like them much recently.

She gunned the engine in her small car and flew like a bat out of hell from the grocery store parking lot. She didn't care that her eggs were squished up against the milk or that the pint of mint chocolate-chip ice cream she had treated herself to was going to melt. She was going to save those boys.

Luckily, all the cops seemed to be elsewhere as she flew up the winding road to Stone Mountain Ranch. Mia racked her brain trying to come up with a valid reason for Grayson and Alexander to be at the ranch. Stone Mountain Ranch was a local horse ranch in the small mountain town of Silver Springs with nothing particularly special about it. It was said to be owned by a billionaire, but that he was almost never there. It was more of a local rumor that a billionaire owned the place than an actual fact. Even the name of the supposed billionaire owner changed based on who was telling the story.

There was no good reason for the boys to be there. Grayson was seven and Alexander was eleven, so they couldn't be looking for work. They'd both been raised in the city with their older sister, Lily, and as far as Mia knew, neither of the boys had a reason to want to see horses. Lily maybe, but not the boys.

Mia stepped down harder on the gas pedal, needing to get to the ranch as quickly as possible. If the police were involved, it would be the end of the small family she had worked so hard to save. Lily and her brothers were on their last foster home. If anything happened, they were going to have to be broken up, and that was the last thing Mia wanted.

A girl was walking alongside the road as it turned to gravel from pavement. Mia slammed on the brakes and skidded slightly on the empty road to come to a stop next to the young woman.

"Lily?" Mia called out, rolling down her window.

Lily coughed and waved away some dust. Her shoulders sagged as she saw who it was. "Hi, Mia."

"What are you doing out here?" Mia asked.

"Going for a walk?" Lily shrugged and offered a fake smile. "You know since I can't drive for another month?"

"Sure. That sounds almost reasonable." Mia shook her head and gave the girl a hard stare. "Get in the car. I've got to pick up your brothers."

Lily's shoulders slumped further as she hurried to the passenger door and got into the car. She belted herself in and stared at her dusty tennis shoes saying nothing.

Mia just put the car back into gear and continued

toward the ranch. One of the big horse barns was visible coming up over the hill. Mia was headed for the main house, though. She had been to the ranch once for a fundraiser, so she at least had some idea where she was going.

"Mia?" Lily bit her lip as dark hair fell across her furrowed brow. "How much trouble are Grayson and Alexander in?"

Mia kept her eyes on the road, looking for the sign that pointed to the main house. "I don't know. I'm hoping to beat the cops there, but I'm about thirty seconds late at this point."

"Cops?" Lily shrank in her seat and wrapped her arms around her small frame.

"Yes, cops," Mia replied. "You were supposed to be watching them."

"I don't know what happened. We were all in the kitchen together, and then they said they were going to watch a movie." Lily shrank a little further into herself as her hair fell further in front of her face. "I came to make sure they weren't watching one of the scary ones that gives Grayson nightmares, but they were gone. They'd left cartoons on so I wouldn't hear them leave."

"And you didn't call me? Or Margie?" Mia asked, frowning at Lily. "Your foster mom should have been the first call."

"Margie was at her bridge game, and you know how hard it's been for her with the three of us in her house," Lily explained. "I didn't want to bother her. I thought I could find them before they got into trouble and no one would ever know."

Mia stopped sharply in front of the big farm house, making both of them lurch in their seats. She turned and looked at Lily. "Cops, Lily. They are going to call the police on your brothers. You should have called me."

"I'm sorry, Mia," Lily said softly, staring at her feet. "Please don't let them take my brothers away from me."

Mia recognized the tone of Lily's voice. Heartbreak with a touch of terror. It nearly broke Mia's heart. The two boys were all Lily had, and Lily was all those boys had. If she were just a few years older, Lily would have taken custody of both of them. Mia knew how hard Lily was working to keep her small family together.

"I'm going to do my best, Lily," Mia promised, putting a hand on the girl's shoulder. "I don't want them to break you up, you know that. I think you need to be together. That's why I got Margie out of retirement to take the three of you when no one else would."

Lily nodded and looked at Mia with big brown eyes. "I know you'll help us, Mia. You're the only one since Gran who has ever helped us."

Mia gave Lily's shoulder a reassuring squeeze and put on a confident smile. "Let's go get your brothers out of trouble."

"Can I come in with you?" Lily asked, her brown eyes fierce. "It's my fault that they were out here."

Mia paused, about to tell her to stay in the car, but she changed her mind. Having Lily as a backup to help keep her brothers calm while Mia dealt with the adults would be useful.

Luckily, the only cars in front of the farmhouse appeared to be security hired by the ranch rather than police cruisers. Mia breathed a small sigh of relief as she walked up to the front door and rang the bell. She squared her shoulders and put on her best 'I'm in charge' face.

The door swung open, revealing a tall man in ranch gear. He was tall and obviously built for hard labor. His plaid shirt hugged his shoulders down to a trim waist with well-worn cowboy boots on his feet. Blue eyes peered at her from a sun-tanned face and wind-whipped dirty blond hair.

"These your boys?" the man asked gruffly, crossing his arms. He opened the door a little wider to reveal Alexander and Grayson sitting nervously on a couch surrounded by four armed guards. It seemed a bit of overkill for an eleven and seven-year-old, but given that this was a billionaire's play ranch, she wasn't too surprised. A billionaire could afford the best.

Mia pushed past the man she assumed was the ranch manager and went straight for the boys. She was glad none of the guards tried to block her path because she was gearing up for Mama Bear mode. Those boys were her priority.

"Are you two okay?" Mia asked, kneeling in front of the two boys. Both were on the smaller side, like their sister, with dark hair and big chocolate brown eyes. When they smiled, Mia was sure they were two of the most handsome men on the planet. They were going to be heart-breakers when they grew up.

Alexander and Grayson both nodded but kept their heads down. She reached out and took their hands to find they were both shaking.

"Ma'am, I'm going to need to call the police," the manager informed her coming up behind her. "They won't talk to me other than to say that I should call you."

Mia squeezed the boys' hands before standing up and facing the manager. If he hadn't called the police yet, there was a good chance that she could sweet talk her way out of this. She was ready to do just about anything to keep this family.

Mia rose to her full height and lifted her chin to meet

the man's gaze head on. He had beautiful blue eyes, but that wasn't about to stop her from making sure these boys went home with their sister and stayed there.

"What are you accusing these boys of?" she asked, putting her hands on her hips.

The man raised a single eyebrow. "Security caught them coming in through the broken window. We have a video of them breaking the window, by the way, as well as coming in and trying to take this statue. They had it in their hands when security got here."

He pointed to the coffee table where a trophy sat. It wasn't very large, with a gold triangular base and a car perched on the top looking like it just slid into the finish line of a race. Something was written on the base, but she couldn't see what it was. It looked rather inexpensive, and certainly not something worth stealing. There were far more valuable items in the richly decorated room worth taking over the statue.

"In their hands?" Mia repeated, suddenly a little less sure of herself. She could feel her righteous fury leaking right out of her like helium out an old balloon.

The man nodded. "They won't tell me why, either."

Mia glanced over at the two boys. They were both sitting with their heads bowed. Alexander had his arm wrapped protectively around his little brother. Lily moved silently away from the door and sat down, so Grayson nestled in between his siblings.

"Let me talk to them," Mia asked, watching the two boys. "There has to be a good reason. They're good kids."

"If you say so," the man said with a shrug. He motioned her toward them, then crossed his big arms and waited.

She took a deep breath before kneeling once again on the floor in front of the kids. She could feel the man's eyes on her back as she reached out and took Grayson's hand in hers to give it a gentle squeeze. Grayson looked up with big, scared eyes. He was about ten seconds away from bursting into tears but was doing his best to stay brave.

"Tell me what happened," Mia softly prompted. "I promise I won't be mad."

Grayson looked helplessly at his older brother. Alexander tightened his embrace around Grayson's shoulders.

"You promise you won't be mad?" Alexander asked.

Mia nodded. "I can't promise you won't be in trouble, but I promise you that I won't be angry. I'll listen, and I'll do what I can to make this better. But you have to tell me what happened or I can't help."

Alexander paused, glancing around the room. One of the security guards looked over and crossed his arms. Alexander swallowed hard.

"The kids at school were teasing Grayson." Alexander looked directly into Mia's eyes, hoping she would understand.

"They said I was a chicken. That I was worthless and that nobody wanted me," Grayson replied. His little voice broke slightly on the word 'worthless,' and it nearly broke Mia's heart.

"You're not worthless," she instantly told him with another hand squeeze. "But what does that have to do with you stealing that trophy?"

"They said I could be in their group if I stole something from the guy that lives here. It had to have his name on it, and that trophy has a name on it," Grayson explained. "They said I was too stupid to actually be able to do it. I guess they were right."

His little face crumpled and a tear trickled down his

cheek. It took everything Mia had not to scoop him up right there, take him home, and go beat up the kids at school herself.

"So you came here to steal the trophy so the kids at school would let you play with them?" Mia confirmed.

Grayson and Alexander nodded slowly.

"I thought if I helped him, he could show it to the kids at school tomorrow and they'd stop teasing him at least," Alexander explained. "It was supposed to be easy."

Mia sighed softly. She wondered what the security guards and the ranch owner thought of all this.

"Did you know about this, Lily?" Mia asked, looking over at their sister.

She shook her head vehemently. "No. I mean, I knew the other kids were giving him a hard time, but I didn't know just how much."

"We didn't tell her because we didn't want her to get in trouble," Alexander quickly explained. "We wanted her to be able to go to a good foster home if we got caught."

"I'm not leaving you guys," Lily told him. She put her arm around Grayson's shoulders over Alexander's arm. "No matter what. We stay together."

Mia swallowed down the heartache growing in her chest. If the cops were called on this, then it wouldn't be Lily's choice. They were out of foster home options for three kids together who had a bad history.

"Okay," Mia said with a sigh. She did her best to smile at the three children who were now depending entirely on her to save them. "Let me go talk with the manager, and we'll see what we can do. Thank you for telling me what was going on."

Three sets of dark eyes watched as she slowly stood and went back to where the tall blond man was waiting for her.

"Mister... I'm afraid I didn't catch your name," Mia apologized as she came to the doorway where he was leaning.

"Carter, ma'am. My name's Carter. And I heard what those boys said," he told her. Something about him softened as he looked over at the kids. He was a good-looking man, with a strong jaw and broad shoulders. He looked a lot calmer and less like a caged tiger now that he had heard the boys' explanation for the broken window.

"Mr. Carter, I know the boys broke your window, but can you please not press charges?" Mia wondered if getting on her knees and begging would help, but decided against it. "They really are good kids. They just need a chance."

Carter looked thoughtful. He glanced over at the window and then back to the boys. He evaluated Mia for a long minute before a slow, small smile spread across his face. Mia couldn't help but notice how the smile seemed to light up his features and turn him from good-looking to devastatingly handsome.

"I won't press charges if they pay for the window," he told her, crossing his arms and looking rather pleased with himself.

Mia glanced at the window. It wasn't exceptionally large or ornate, but it certainly cost more than a couple of foster kids with no money to their names had to spend.

"Um, we would be happy to take you up on the offer, but they don't exactly have a lot of money right now," she explained. In her head, she started mentally checking her own bank account balance to see if she could swing it herself.

"I'll take sweat payment," Carter told her. "There's always things that need to be done around here. They can earn the window by doing jobs here."

"You'd let them do that?" Mia asked, surprised at his generosity.

"I would," he told her with that same slow smile. "They're just kids in a bad situation. You said to give them a chance. That's what I'm doing."

Mia nearly hugged the man. "I'll go tell them," she told him. "You won't regret this."

"I'm sure I will regret it, but it's the right thing to do." He let out a wry chuckle as she turned and went to kneel before the kids again.

"Okay, he's agreed not to call the police, but you have to pay back the window. You can earn the cost of the window back by working here," she told Alexander and Grayson.

"We can do that," Alexander promised her immediately.

"I'm good with horses," Grayson informed her. "I'll ride them and get them to do stuff like they do at the circus."

"I doubt he'll have you working too much with them," Mia replied with a gentle smile. The idea of the scrawny seven-year-old training a thousand pound animal to do tricks wasn't quite the work she imagined they'd be doing.

"I'll help too," Lily announced.

"You didn't break the window, Lily," Mia reminded her.

"No, but I was supposed to be watching them," she replied. "Besides, if I help, they'll earn it back faster."

"Okay." Mia looked at the three, suddenly hopeful children in front of her. "So you'll work here to pay for the window? It's a deal?"

All three nodded enthusiastically.

"Excellent," Carter said, coming up behind Mia.

She stood up quickly, nearly colliding with him in the process. He reached out a hand to steady her as she stepped back. His touch was strong yet gentle at the same time.

"Thank you," she said, feeling her cheeks heat slightly,

but she wasn't about to let it get to her. "They've agreed to work for you, Mr. Carter."

"Carter is my first name," he told her. "And I'm happy to have them. And you, Ms. Amesworth."

"Me?" Mia frowned slightly. "What do you mean?"

Carter motioned to the children. "They're going to need some supervision. You're part of this bargain, too."

Mia opened her mouth and then shut it. She didn't want to wreck this deal for her kids. She would come up with a way to make it work. Maybe she could get the foster mom to come help, or even bring her laptop and get work done while she was here.

"I'll make it work, I guess," Mia replied. She held out her hand. "Do we have a deal?"

Carter's big hand wrapped around hers. It was warm and strong. "We have a deal."

Chapter 2

arter

CARTER WATCHED as the small car with the woman and three children drove off his ranch. He shook his head, wondering how in the world that woman was planning on managing those kids. They'd all signed non-disclosure agreements and were supposed to come back the following Monday to start work. He hoped it would go well.

They seemed nice enough, as far as kids went. Carter didn't have much experience with anyone under eighteen, but they seemed well behaved once they were in custody. He could certainly understand and even relate to their actions, but they were still kids. Troubles and liabilities all rolled into one cute package.

"And that's why I'm never having any," he mumbled under his breath to no one in particular. One of the security guards raised an eyebrow at him but didn't say anything.

"So, what's the damage?" Carter asked, walking over to his head of security.

To say that Brian was a big man would be an understatement. Brian Cards was a giant of a man who could shoot the legs off a fly at one hundred yards. The man was deadly and incredibly good at keeping people alive. That's why he was in charge of Carter's security.

"It looks as if it really was just two kids sneaking in," Brian replied. He motioned to the window. "If anything, this was an effective drill. It just shows us that we need to up our response time. I think we can shave another thirty seconds off."

Carter nodded. His heart was finally starting to come back to a regular rhythm after hearing the alarms go off all over the ranch. He had been sure it was the person who had been sending death threats to his office. He'd moved to his secret ranch to get away from them only a few days ago. This ranch was now his home. It was where he was supposed to be safe.

"We'll get this window cleaned up and replaced," Brian told him. "But, just to be on the safe side, I'd like to have an extra man on patrol for the next couple of days."

Carter nodded. "That's fine with me."

"Why do you think those kids tried to steal this?" Brian asked, picking up the trophy and handing it to Carter.

It was a nice little trophy. It had a good weight to it, and the sculpture of the car cast in some sort of fake golden metal was certainly pleasing, but it wasn't worth much. It was also fifteen years old, so any worth it did had was long evaporated. The title of "Best Car Design, Carter Williamson" decorated the bottom. It wasn't the dollar value of the trophy, but that it was the first step he'd taken to starting his business that was valuable. Carter owned socks worth more than the cost of the actual trophy.

"To show it off," Carter said, carefully polishing the car with his shirt cuff before putting it back up on his mantel. It needed dusting. "To say that they were bad-ass enough to sneak into a billionaire's home and steal something."

"I guess that could make a kid cool," Brian agreed. He shook his head and looked out at the now empty road. "And it seems like those two kids could use some cool in their life."

"What makes you say that?" Carter asked.

"Did you see their clothes? Second hand. Their shoes? Worn thin," Brian explained. "The woman that came and picked them up? She was a social worker, not their mom or aunt or anything. Those kids are in the system. No wonder the younger one was getting picked on."

"So you don't think there was any reason not to believe them?" Carter asked. He hated feeling this nervous, but this was the first break-in at the property. This was supposed to be his safe place, and after what had happened at his office, he was afraid to take any chances.

"I believe them, all of it," Brian assured him. "They were too scared to have anyone telling them what to do. The break-in was all them. You're safe here, sir."

"Good." Carter swallowed his nerves. To anyone watching, he was calm and collected, but deep in his chest the threads of anxiety were still strung tightly. The close calls had him rattled.

"Don't worry, sir," Brian said. "We'll make sure that whoever is sending you death threats isn't going to succeed."

Carter nodded. "Thank you, Brian."

Brian nodded and motioned to his men. They cleared out of Carter's living room and headed out the front door.

Carter listened to them set up their posts outside, the sounds of their walkie-talkies never quite fading away.

Carter looked at the trophy on the mantel and wondered what the boys would have done with it after they showed it to their friends. The first thing that popped in his mind was that they would have returned it. Or, rather, the woman-their social worker, would have made them return it.

Mia. The name was short and sweet, like her. He usually liked his women leggy and blonde, which Mia was neither. But there was definitely something about her that attracted her to him. She was full of fire and passion. He could practically still smell the smoke from the flames coming out of her eyes as she protected those boys.

He rather hoped he'd be seeing more of her. He had a sneaking suspicion that she wouldn't let those boys out of her sight for a moment and the idea of her on his ranch made him smile. He was a little surprised at how the idea of having her around lightened his heart. There was just something about Mia that intrigued him.

He looked out the broken window at the mountains and his ranch. He hoped that working here would give the boys confidence to stand up for themselves. As a kid, he'd been scrawny and nerdy, so all the local bullies had pushed him around too. It had been someone taking a moment to teach him how to work with horses that had turned him into the man he was today, so it was time to pass that gift on.

Carter looked over at his trophy one last time before deciding to go to the barn. He wanted to do something with his hands, something that would keep his fingers busy and his mind off the threats hanging around him and his car company. He had the option of working on one of his cars or working with the horses of his ranch. He decided horses would be the better company.

With a shake of his head to clear his thoughts, he turned and headed to the barn. He let his mind drift to what he would have the boys and their sister do to earn back the cost of the window. He already had plans for them and their fiery guardian.

Chapter 3

M *ia*

"MAYBE WE'LL GET to ride the horses like cowboys," Grayson shouted, bouncing around in the backseat. His seat belt was barely holding him down in his booster seat, and Mia had already asked him three times to remember to stay seated. He was just too excited to contain himself.

Mia pulled up to the big ranch house, this time invited rather than coming to rescue her boys. All three kids were in the car, and all three of them were jabbering ideas of what they thought they were going to do.

"I have a feeling it will be more like mucking stalls, or cleaning or something," Mia said gently as she put the car in park. The kids all opened their doors and rushed out into the country air.

It smelled like clean air, grass, and... horses. Definitely, like horses. It wasn't a bad scent, but it wasn't something that Mia wanted to wear as perfume either.

Definitely doing something with cleaning the stalls.... she thought as she caught the main scent coming from the big barn to her left.

"Glad you all made it," Carter called out, coming out of the barn to greet them. He was wearing perfectly worn jeans, a navy T-shirt, and a baseball cap. He looked good. Really good. Mia had to force her eyes away to stop looking him over, so she checked her watch once again, just to make sure they were on time. They had arrived five minutes early just in case. There was no way Mia was going to risk anything with these kids.

All three of the children ran over to stand in front of him. Alexander's foot tapped nervously, but otherwise, they all had big hopeful grins plastered across their faces. Carter appraised them for a moment.

"This is Laura," Carter told them as a young woman came out to stand next to him. She was probably only a couple of years younger than Mia. Her dark red hair was pulled back into a ponytail, and her green eyes sparkled as she smiled at the kids.

"Hi," she greeted them. She stepped forward and made sure to shake each of their hands as if they were adults. It made Mia like her instantly since she treated her kids with respect.

"Laura will be your boss," Carter informed them. "If she says jump, you just jump. Don't even ask how high. That's how in charge she is."

"Yes, sir," all three children replied like miniature soldiers. Grayson even did a pretend salute. Mia could only imagine he'd seen it done like that in a movie.

Laura chuckled and knelt down in front of Grayson.

"I have a little brother and sister about your age," Laura told him. Her green eyes met his, and her face went serious. "If you're going to help me, I need to see your muscles."

Grayson frowned, not understanding. He looked over at Mia, but Mia just shrugged.

"Like this," Alexander explained, flexing his arm and showing his bicep. Grayson copied the movement and made a growling noise as he made his muscles bigger.

Laura reached over and felt the muscle. "Whoa! You might be too strong," she said, looking impressed.

Grayson grinned at her and puffed his chest out with pride.

"Okay, then." Laura stood up and put her hand on Grayson's shoulder to guide him toward the large barn. "Let's head into the stables and get started. We have a lot to do today."

All three children willingly followed Laura through the large double doors. Mia hung back for a moment.

"Mr. Carter?" Mia approached him, tucking a strand of hair behind her ear. Now that they were alone, she was suddenly nervous. She wasn't good with very attractive men and never knew how to behave around them.

"It's just Carter," he told her with an easy smile.

"I just wanted to thank you again," Mia said quickly. She smiled nervously. "Thank you for giving my boys another chance."

"You're welcome." He smiled again, easy and confident as he leaned toward her slightly. "Want to see what they're up to?"

"I'd love to." She grinned and nodded as they started walking together toward the open barn doors.

"So, how did you get to be in charge of the trouble makers?" he asked as they approached the entrance.

"I'm their social worker," Mia explained. "They were assigned to me."

"You seem to care an awful lot for a social worker," Carter remarked. He paused slightly by the door and held it open for her. She looked over at him. He had an open face and an honesty to his eyes that told Mia he didn't mean any harm by the comment.

"I do care a lot about them," she said slowly, doing her best not to be defensive. She probably cared more than she should about them, but that wasn't something he needed to know. "They're good kids."

"You say that a lot," he replied.

Mia glared at him for a moment. "That's because it's true. They are."

He nodded as they entered the barn.

The smell of horse and hay was stronger inside. The stalls were large and spacious with plenty of storage room off to the side. Mia didn't know much about horses, but she knew a stable like this had to be top of the line. It was nicer and certainly bigger than her apartment.

Inside, Grayson was already up to his elbows in soapy water leaning over what Mia assumed was a watering trough. He had on yellow gloves that were about six sizes too big, but with a grin to match as he scrubbed. Alexander and Lily were in one of the stalls, both with shovels. Despite the smell coming from that particular stall, they both were laughing.

"Make sure to get all of it," Laura advised, standing off to the side and observing.

Mia leaned against the door frame and watched her kids. They were happy, and it made her heart swell. This was going to be good for them. All of them. They wanted so badly to please, and here, they could really feel useful.

"They look like they're going to do a good job," Carter said, watching the kids work under Laura's watchful eyes.

Mia nodded, watching as Alexander enthusiastically scooped a very large load of something Mia didn't want to think about out of the stall.

"Gonna be sore tomorrow, though," Carter said with a laugh as he watched the boy struggle to balance the shovel without spilling it.

Mia laughed. "That load's nearly as big as he is."

Carter's laugh was low and musical. It made Mia want to laugh along with him without needing a joke. She turned, and their eyes met. He had such a great smile. Friendly. Warm.

"How long have you worked here?" Mia asked, doing her best not to get lost in his eyes. "I don't think I've seen you in town, and it's not that big of a town."

Carter shrugged. "I've been with the ranch for a long time, but I've never been able to stay as long as I'd like here."

Mia's brows came together as she tried to figure out what Carter did at the ranch that allowed him to leave and come back like that. "I guess I should ask what your job is then. I thought you were the ranch manager, but..."

Carter looked puzzled at her for a moment. "Laura is the ranch manager."

"So, what's your job?" Mia asked, trying to think of another job that would put him in charge without having to be in town all the time.

A slow smile filled Carter's face, and his eyes started to sparkle. He chuckled, enjoying his new secret. "If you haven't figured it out yet, I'm not going to tell you."

Mia crossed her arms and glared at him, but it just made him chuckle again. Apparently, he wasn't as intimidated by her "tell me now" stare as her kids were.

Fine, she thought, turning away from him. *I'll just look him up later. I've got pretty good Google skills.*

"Laura, will we get to work with the horses today?" Lily asked Laura, drawing Mia's attention.

Laura shook her head. "Not today. I needed to see what you knew how to do. Next time we'll work with the animals."

Lily looked crestfallen, but then quickly picked up her shovel and grinned. She waved to Mia and went into the next stall, ready to earn her place at the ranch.

"Would you like a tour of the ranch?" Carter asked Mia.

She turned, surprised by his question. He stood in the doorway, all sexy jeans and easy smile and for a moment, Mia completely forgot how to speak.

"Um, don't I need to watch them?" she finally managed to get out, stumbling over every word. "You know, make sure you're getting your money's worth?"

Carter chuckled. "I'm sure Laura will make sure that they are working hard and being safe," he assured her. "Tour?"

Her bottom lip was between her teeth as she hesitated for just a moment. She glanced over to see Laura showing Alexander a better way to shovel and telling Grayson he was doing a great job.

"Okay, I'll take your tour," Mia said, putting a smile on her face. It would be fun. Maybe she'd even get some hints to his identity.

"Excellent," Carter replied, a grin filling his handsome features. "I'll give you the twenty-five-cent version."

"Isn't it usually a 'ten-cent' tour?" Mia asked, puzzled as she followed him out of the barn.

Carter winked at her. "My tour is worth the extra charge."

Chapter 4

arter

CARTER WASN'T EXACTLY sure what had prompted him to offer Mia a tour. There were a million things that he needed to do, and walking a social worker around the ranch wasn't one of them. Yet, now that he had made the offer, he found he was actually excited to show her around. He was curious what she was going to think of the place.

He took a step back from the big barn doors and motioned grandly to them. "Here, we have the barn and the stables."

She laughed, her nose crinkling slightly and her eyes sparkling. The sunlight hit her light brown hair and made it gleam. It caught him by surprise, and he lost his train of thought for a moment. She was beautiful. She turned her smile onto him, and his stomach tightened with desire and something much deeper.

"Where are all the horses?" she asked, glancing about. "I didn't see any in there."

"They're out in the pasture while it's still nice out," he replied. He motioned off toward the paddocks. "You want to see them?"

She nodded eagerly. "They're part of the tour, right?"

"The best part," he assured her, feeling a smile fill his face. He was glad he'd asked her to go on this tour. If she kept up this level of enthusiasm, it would be an enjoyable way to spend the afternoon. It was always nice to show things to someone who enjoyed them.

"We'll walk through the arena to get to Paddock Number Three." He motioned to the large building connected to the stables and started walking toward the small side door leading inside.

The air was slightly cooler inside the arena. It was a huge space that was used for training and exercising the horses when the weather was bad. The scent of clean wood and fresh water filled the building. He could hear the three kids' laughter echoing in from the attached stables.

"This is nice," Mia remarked. She was looking around; her arms wrapped loosely around her torso. She smiled and shrugged at him. He picked up his pace slightly, wanting to get her to a part of the tour she would really appreciate. He wanted to see her smile light up the room again.

"So, what's the kids' story?" Carter asked, opening up the door to head outside. "How'd they end up with you making sure they pay for broken windows?"

"Because I'm the best," she replied, giving him a confident smile that made him like her more.

"Is that so?"

She nodded. "I asked for this case. It's a hard one, but I wanted to help." She looked out at the mountains and sighed. "They didn't have anyone. Their mom abandoned them, and they've gotten into some trouble in the past. Mostly running away and having issues with authority, but it makes their record look bad. When I got them, the state was getting ready to split them up."

Carter thought of how the older brother had tried to help little Grayson. Granted, breaking into his ranch wasn't the best idea, but it showed love. "The last thing those kids need is to be apart," he said.

"No kidding," Mia agreed. "I took their case because I knew I could keep them together. They deserve a good life. So, thank you for helping them. It really means a lot."

She smiled up at him, blushed, and then hurried along the path toward the open space. It was a quick walk through the arena to the paddock. The sun had come out from behind a cloud, illuminating the beautiful mountain views. Three paddocks nestled around the barn and arena for the horses to graze and be outside. They then gave way to wild meadow-lands that rose into foothills leading to the craggy mountains.

The breeze ruffled her hair, and she tucked it shyly behind an ear as they walked. It was still warm enough to be comfortable, but the wind coming down off the mountains had the smell of snow. It wouldn't be long before winter arrived.

Carter leaned against the wooden fence and put his fingers in his mouth. He blew out one long, loud, and clear whistle and was secretly pleased with how Mia's eyebrows raised at the sound. It was childish, but he was rather proud of his ability to whistle.

Five horse heads perked up from the meadow and looked in their direction. Carter whistled again, this time adding in a short burst at the end for emphasis. Four of the

horses went back to grazing, but the fifth started to obedi-
ently trot over.

Mia watched with wide eyes as his beautiful white mare
came to the fence. The mare nuzzled Carter's hands,
searching for sugar cubes or treats.

"She's beautiful," Mia whispered. Carter had to agree.

"You can pet her," Carter said. He reached up and
scratched the mare's soft white neck. "She's very friendly."

Mia approached the fence slowly, her smile growing as
she came closer. "I haven't been around horses since I was
young," she told him.

She walked up to the fence next to Carter and stepped
on a loose rock. Her balance wobbled, and she grabbed at
the fence. He reached out to steady her, his hand going to
the small of her back. Touching her sent heat coursing
through his body that he wasn't expecting.

She regained her balance and chuckled, shrugging off
the mishap with a smile. He had to force himself to let go of
her since his hand didn't want to leave her body. She smiled
up at him before reaching out her hand for the horse to
smell. The mare presented her soft neck for Mia to touch.

"Her name is Hopeful Dreamer," he told her as the mare
nickered softly and bumped her nose against his shoulder.
She still wanted a treat for coming when called. He reached
into his pocket and pulled out a sugar cube. "Here," he told
Mia. "You can give it to her."

Mia's face lit up like a little kid's, and again he felt a
warmth fill his core. Her excitement was contagious, and he
loved getting to share in it. She grinned a little wider and
held out her hand for the sugar cube before offering it palm
up to Hopeful Dreamer.

Hopeful delicately took the treat like the lady she was. Mia
giggled and turned to face him. The wind caught her hair, and

she brushed it out of the way, her eyes dancing. Her face was alight with excitement, and the beauty of it took him off guard for a moment. She was stunningly attractive, and cute when she was angry, but when she smiled, she was downright stunning.

"She's beautiful," Mia told him, her eyes and smile going back to the horse.

"Thank you," he replied. Hopeful shifted her body parallel to the fence so that Carter could scratch her rump. The horse leaned into his hand as he scratched her white coat.

Mia copied the motion and laughed as Hopeful groaned with pleasure. "She's like a big puppy."

Carter laughed and moved his hand to a better scratching spot just as Mia did. Their hands collided, sending another jolt of heat straight through him. Mia's cheeks pinked slightly, and he had to look away so that he wouldn't stare.

The pink suited her and made his thoughts drift to other things that would pink her cheeks.

"How did you get into this?" Mia asked, carefully petting the horse again. "Horses, I mean."

Carter looked out at the mountains, his gaze going distant as he remembered. "When I was about Alexander's age, I got into some trouble. My uncle decided that I needed to learn what hard work was and made me work on his ranch."

Mia's head cocked slightly as she looked up at him. "This sounds like a familiar story..."

"Maybe a little." Carter chuckled. "I hated it at first. It was hard work, but then I grew to love it. These animals, they grow on you."

Mia nodded. "I can believe that." She laughed as

Hopeful moved closer to get more scratches. Mia happily obliged.

Carter smiled. "Hopeful Dreamer is my favorite mare here. She's gentle, smart, and an excellent mother."

"She's definitely friendly," Mia agreed. She motioned to the mare's extended belly. "Is she pregnant now?"

Carter nodded. "Due in the next few weeks."

Mia frowned and Carter had to resist the temptation to reach out and smooth the crease from her brow. He liked her smiling much better than frowning.

"Do horses usually have babies in the fall?"

"No," Carter said, shaking his head. "Foaling is usually in the spring or summer, so this is pretty late. She had some artificial help."

Hopeful Dreamer looked at the two of them and made a low huff sound. They'd both stopped scratching her, and she wanted more. Mia laughed and went back to scratching her rump. Hopeful's eyes closed with pleasure.

"I don't know much about horses. I had a few riding lessons as a kid, but..." Mia shrugged. "Do you know if the baby will be a boy or a girl?"

Carter's fingers untangled a long white lock of mane as he stroked the mare. "We'll find out when it's born." He smiled at her. "You had riding lessons?"

"Yeah." She looked at him, then at the horse, then back to him. "You don't really want to know my life's story. I'm sure it's not terribly interesting."

"It is to me."

"Okay." She seemed to evaluate him for a moment as if deciding whether he was telling the truth or not. He grinned at her. She apparently liked it and decided he was really interested. "My mom had some issues, and I've never met my father. I was put into foster care when I was six. It wasn't exactly a happy childhood."

"I'm sorry to hear that," he said softly. She shrugged as if it didn't bother her, but he could see her in a new light. She fought for her kids because she knew exactly what it was like to be one. Her strength impressed him.

"When I was ten, I moved to a new foster house. The neighbors had a horse, and that summer, they gave me lessons." Mia slowly pat Dreamer, as if the motion soothed her while she remembered. A slow smile came across her face. "It's probably one of the best memories I have."

"Do you still ride?" Carter asked, watching her. She had such pain inside of her. He didn't know what made her so special, but all he wanted to do was wrap his arms around her and protect her from everything. He wished he could somehow give her a different, happier, childhood.

"No," she said, shaking her head. "The horse was sold that fall, so it didn't last long. I never really had the opportunity again."

"You didn't ask for more lessons?" he asked.

"Oh, I asked," she told him. "But I was a foster kid. There's barely enough money to keep a kid clothed, let alone get them expensive lessons." She let out a mirthless chuckle. "I stopped asking after a while."

Something inside his heart squeezed tight.

"Do you want to go for a ride sometime?" he asked, the question popping out before he had time to think about it.

She looked up at him surprised. "Seriously?"

"I'm always serious," he informed her.

"That would be nice," she replied with a smile. "I'd love to get back on a horse. Thank you."

"It's a date, then," he replied. He loved the way her cheeks pinked again.

"I meant, with the kids," she stammered. "Because that's why I'm here."

"Of course," he promised. "Whatever you want."

Mia looked up at him and opened her mouth to say something, but was interrupted before she got the words out. He internally cursed whoever was interrupting them. He was enjoying this time with her.

"Mia?" Lily called out as she came over, her eyes lighting up at the sight of the horse. "Laura says that's all she has for us today."

"Already?" Mia sounded surprised. She glanced down at her watch and did a double take. "That went fast."

Carter checked his own watch to see that an hour and a half had already passed. It had felt like only seconds with Mia.

"Okay, I'll be right there," Mia told Lily. She pulled her hand away from the horse and turned to face Carter directly. "Thank you for the tour. I'd love to see the rest of the place sometime."

"I'd like that very much," he assured her. Her cheeks flushed slightly as she smiled, and he liked the way it looked on her. She was open and easy to read, which was rare in Carter's world. Despite knowing her for less than two days, he trusted this woman and found himself looking forward to running into her again. His first impression of her had been right.

She hesitated for a moment, and Carter hoped it was because she didn't want to leave.

"I guess we'll see you next time," she said. She smiled and then quickly went to join Lily. She put her arm around the younger girl's shoulder and together they walked into the barn.

Carter turned back to Hopeful Dreamer and smiled as

he shook his head. He'd enjoyed their conversation more than he'd expected. It flowed easily, not to mention she was easy on the eyes.

"A woman is the last thing you need right now," he told himself quietly. He would leave the ranch as soon as the threats stopped. For all he knew, things could be wrapped up and his need to be here gone by the end of the week.

For the first time since his arrival, he found himself hoping he got to stay longer. He was already looking forward to the next visit.

"It's a bad idea," he said to himself. "I should stay away from her."

Hopeful Dreamer looked up at him and huffed a contrary opinion as she looked at her new friend.

"Right, because a romantic tie to the woman whose kids broke into my house is a good idea," he told the horse. "Especially with everything else going on."

He could have sworn Hopeful rolled her eyes at him and shrugged. Yet, somehow, he found himself agreeing with the horse.

Chapter 5

*M*ia

"I've got the kids, Margie, so you go to your doctor's appointment and take your time," Mia said into her phone as she pulled up to the school pick up/drop off area. She was about ten minutes early, but that was good since it meant she got a better spot.

"Thanks, Mia," Margie, the kids' foster mother told her. "I know this wasn't the plan. This was the only time my doctor could see me, though."

"The plan was for you to take these kids because no one else would. I pulled you out of retirement because I was desperate for these kids to have one more chance," Mia replied. Margie had been one of Mia's best foster parents before she retired and Mia had begged her to come back. "You were the only person I knew of that would take three kids out of the blue. Especially three troubled kids on the verge of being separated."

"I just wish I were younger so I could keep up with them better," Margie said, sounding glum. "You were right. They're good kids."

Mia smiled. "You're doing more than I could have ever asked, so thank you."

"You be careful, Mia," Margie warned. "I know how attached to your charges you get. I don't want you to get hurt. They aren't your kids. They're the system's. You're going above and beyond for these kids, and I don't want you to burn out."

Mia sighed. "I know. It's just the situation. I would do this much work for any of my kids." In her mind's eye, Mia could see the disapproving look Margie was giving her.

"If you say so," Margie replied. "I just don't want you getting too attached and having your heart broken."

"Thank you," Mia told her, trying not to take Margie's concern personally. "You go to your doctor appointment as planned. I'll take them to the ranch and get them some dinner. You make sure that doctor gives you a new hip or something so you can keep up with these kids."

Margie laughed, and they both hung up with smiles.

Mia checked her watch. She was still early for the bell, so she took out her phone and pulled up Google. It was time to find out more about Carter and that stupid smile when she didn't recognize him was about.

"Carter and Stone Mountain Ranch," she murmured as she typed in the search bar. She hit enter, not expecting much.

Nothing came up. The only hit was for the address of the ranch, which wasn't even correctly labeled on the map. It felt a little weird, like someone had manipulated the search results.

Mia frowned slightly and tried again. She didn't think

the trophy was Carter's, but it was something worth putting in the search bar. She didn't really have very many other ideas. "Carter and car award."

This time, her eyeballs nearly fell out of their sockets.

He wasn't the manager or some ranch hand or random hired help. He was Carter Williamson, owner and CEO of W Motors, makers of the fastest electric cars on the planet. She'd assumed he was a random employee, but instead, *he* was the freaking billionaire owner.

Mia sank down a little lower in her very worn seat as she scanned his bio. She skimmed the article, trying to read it as quickly as possible before the kids got out of school.

 Carter Wagner Williamson (born 18 July) is an American business magnate, investor, engineer, and philanthropist. He is the founder, CEO and product architect of W Motors as well as several other smaller companies. As of March, he has an estimated net worth of $14.8 billion, making him one of the top 100 wealthiest people in the world.

Due to a recent lawsuit, the safety of the airbags in W Motors came under question. Several owners were injured, and one woman killed when the airbags failed to deploy properly during accidents. It was found that the owners had made modifications to their cars that caused the airbags to malfunction. W Motors was found innocent of all charges, but Carter Williamson still replaced all the affected airbags to make sure his cars remained safe despite no court order to do so.

Stock prices surged after the announcement,

and yet again W Motors is the favorite to win the
Safest Car award for the fifth year in a row.

Mia swallowed hard and continued to read through the article as quickly as she could.

 Williamson has never married. He has stated in
several interviews that he does not wish to have
children.

In addition to helping to design the cars he
manufactures, Williamson is also known for
raising horses. He spent time on his uncle's farm as
a child and has stated that the experience is one
that shapes how he views the world.

In addition to properties in New York City, Los
Angeles, and San Francisco, Williamson owns a
working ranch in Tennessee, three beach houses in
various locations, a home in California, and
several yachts. Many of these are rented out to
charity organizations when not in use.

Mia groaned softly. The article didn't mention any property in Colorado, but that just meant he had so many properties they couldn't list them all. He owned over a dozen properties, but the one her kids broke into was the one he was living at. Just her luck.

The picture in the article was most definitely him. Only, instead of the jeans, t-shirt, and boots, she was used to seeing him in, he was wearing a really, really nice suit. Suits were usually her preferred look for guys, but for some reason, she preferred the jeans on him. It suited him better to her mind.

She shook her head and reread the article. This belonged in some sort of novel, not her real life. Billionaires were like royalty. You saw them in magazines and on TV, wondered what their life would be, and never actually met them. The idea that a billionaire had her kids working on his ranch to pay off a broken window was crazy.

At least it explained the security around the ranch. She'd never seen so many guards responding to a broken window before. However, it being a billionaire's window, it made sense that the response would be rapid and heavy.

The school bell rang, making her look up from her phone. She shook her head and put the phone back in her pocket as a stream of kids poured from the school doors. It was only a few moments before all three kids were in the car and buckling themselves up.

"It's ranch day!" Grayson shrieked, pulling the seat belt across his lap enthusiastically with Alexander's help. Both boys were already grinning from ear to ear with excitement.

Lily wore a matching grin as she settled herself in the front seat. Mia loved that they were all in a good mood. It was such a nice shift from two weeks ago when picking them up from school was like going to a funeral. The ranch was good for them.

"Did you know who Carter is?" Mia asked as everyone buckled up.

"Yeah, he's Carter Williamson, the guy who owns W Motors and makes those awesome cars," Alexander replied. "I didn't know it was his house when we went there, but it makes sense."

Mia just stared at him for a moment. Alexander was completely fine that Carter owned one of the largest car companies in the US and that they were earning back a broken window from him.

"He asked us not to say anything," Lily said from the front seat. "He's trying to keep a low profile, so we're just to tell people Grayson got caught by security, and we're working for Laura. No one even cared, to be honest."

Mia didn't know what to say. The kids all took it in stride who they were working for. She, on the other hand, was still trying to wrap her head around it. She decided that the kids just didn't understand just how much Carter was worth and that they saw him as an equal, not different. If they could do it, then so could she, she decided. He could be a normal, regular guy to her.

Except, when she thought of his blue eyes, she knew that he was anything but normal. And it wasn't his bank account that told her that.

THE THREE KIDS chattered excitedly as Mia drove them to the ranch. She let them talk without interruption, listening to their conversation and chiming in only when they asked her a question. They were there in the space of what felt like only several hundred questions, which was faster than Mia expected.

"Laura said I get to groom the horses today," Alexander announced proudly.

"She said we *all* get to help groom today," Lily corrected him.

"Do I have to?" Grayson asked. He shifted nervously in his booster seat. "Horses are really big."

"You don't have to touch them if you don't want to." Alexander reached over and gently squeezed his arm. "But I want to. It'll be cool."

Grayson chewed on the inside of his lip and nodded. He didn't look completely convinced at the coolness of horses yet.

"This is going to be so awesome," Lily said, getting out of the car. She went and opened the back door up and helped Grayson out.

"You know this is supposed to be work, right?" Mia asked, jokingly. "This is supposed to be a punishment for breaking the window."

"'If you love what you do, you'll never work a day in your life,'" Lily quoted.

"Who taught you that?" Mia asked, impressed.

"You did," Lily told her with a grin. "You said it to me one time at the courthouse when I asked you why you did what you do."

Mia's heart swelled. She hurried over and gave the teenage girl a big hug.

"You three aren't work," she said. Alexander and Grayson ran past her, knocking her off balance. She shook her head and added, "most of the time."

Lily hurried after her brothers with Mia close behind. The two boys and their sister ran to the stables, eager to start their work with the horses. Laura greeted them with big smiles and motioned them over to one of the stables. She made sure she had all three kids' attentions before beginning a lecture on proper grooming techniques.

Mia smiled as she watched them. Laura was amazing with all three of them but was especially attentive to Lily. Laura answered every question with enthusiasm and would tell the teenager why she was doing things so that Lily could learn the thought processes herself. It looked as though Lily had found a new role model, and to be honest, Mia couldn't be happier.

"If I didn't know better, I'd think they were enjoying themselves."

Mia smiled at the now familiar voice. She had so hoped Carter would show up today. Her stomach did a single, excited flip as she turned around.

It was as if he had planned her being in that exact spot to look at him. He stood before her in soft jeans that hugged his frame and a t-shirt that showed just how broad and strong his shoulders were. The sun haloed his golden hair and made him look like some sort of god from a Greek story.

"As far as punishment goes, they are enjoying this far too much," she replied. Her heart fluttered as he came and stood next to her, close enough for her to almost be able to touch him.

He shook his head and grinned. "Sadists."

Mia laughed. How was it that her day suddenly seemed so amazing? Up until this point, it had been a normal day, but if someone had asked, it was now a great day.

"Would you like to finish our tour?" he asked. His lips went to a sexy half-smile as he waited for her response.

She glanced over at the kids, but they had completely forgotten about everything but the horses. Grayson was standing off to the side as the other two started grooming a horse under Laura's watchful eyes. He still looked unsure about being near the big animals, so Mia was glad Laura wasn't pushing him. He yawned, but then went to fetch a brush for his older siblings.

She knew they'd be fine. She chuckled to herself. As if they'd do anything to jeopardize their time here. The ranch and the horses were all they talked about.

"I'd love to," Mia told Carter. "I want to see the rest."

Carter's face split into a grin, and he looked around, figuring out where they left off last time. "You've seen the stables and the arena..."

"And I met Hopeful Dreamer," Mia added.

"Then you need to see the garage. And the house." He paused and looked at her. "Which one would you like first?"

"I'll take the garage, Mr. Williamson," Mia replied, feeling a little bit smug. He raised his eyebrows at her, and she confidently crossed her arms and raised her chin.

"You figured out who I am."

"I did."

"You seem rather calm about it," he said with a knowing smile.

"I had the drive over to stop screaming."

Carter chuckled. It was still hard to believe the man was a billionaire. He seemed so normal. He was still easy to talk to, and that smile of his was still just as disarming.

"So, what's it like owning W Motors?" she asked. "Do you really make as many cars as they say you do?"

He motioned to the path, and they started walking. Together they walked with easy steps along the carefully maintained rock path toward the big garage. It was located on the opposite side of the house from the barn, but it was so beautiful outside that Mia enjoyed the short walk.

"It's a lot of work," Carter said, answering her earlier question. "My father started out making cars and taught me everything I know. Eventually, I started making my own car designs, and that led to building my own company. Cars are in my blood. I love them."

"And here I thought horses were in your blood," Mia replied, motioning to the beautiful horse ranch behind them.

"Horses, horsepower- they're not that different," he explained. His voice warmed with excitement about the topic, and it made her smile. "Cars are what I make. Horses are what I take care of. Both get me where I want to go. I am allowed to enjoy multiple things."

He gently pushed her shoulder in a friendly teasing manner. At his touch, her stomach filled with butterflies again. She secretly hoped he'd do it again, but they were already at the garage.

The garage looked more like a second barn than a traditional garage. The building was huge and made of weathered gray wood, but Mia could see security cameras tucked in the eaves. This was far more than just a regular garage.

"Everything you see in here falls under the non-disclosure agreement you signed the other day," Carter said as they approached the door. "You can't tell people what I'm working on in here."

"Of course," Mia replied. "Besides, who would I tell? Who would even believe me?"

Carter chuckled and went to the door leading inside, but he paused before opening it. "I'm actually working on something, and I'd love your opinion on it. If you're interested."

"On a car?" Mia shrugged. "I'm not exactly a car expert. I'm not sure how much of an opinion I'll have."

"We'll see." He opened the door, and they stepped inside.

Chapter 6

arter

THE INSIDE of the garage was cool and dark after the bright sunshine outside. Mia had to blink several times to adjust to the dimmer lighting as she stepped through the doors. As soon as her eyes could focus, she gasped.

Three sports cars were tucked neatly off to the side. She didn't know exactly what they were, but she recognized them from posters she'd seen over boys' beds during her home checks. She knew enough to know that these were dream cars and probably worth more than six years of her salary.

The center of the room was set up just like her local mechanic's shop. There was a deep pit like what the oil change people used and a huge selection of tools. A bright red sports car was being worked on that she recognized from yet another boy's dream car poster.

"Wow," she whispered, looking around at the expensive cars.

"Oh, not those." Carter shrugged as if they were nothing. "This is what I want your opinion on."

He put his hand on the small of her back and guided her to a far corner of the room. There was a drafting table and a pedestal with a small model of a car resting on it. She found herself missing his touch when he let go of her back.

"This is a prototype I'm working on," he explained. He activated the drafting table, and Mia realized that it was actually a giant digital screen as big as a table. He pulled up some design specs.

"How do you have time to work on a prototype? Aren't you busy managing the company?" Mia asked.

Carter shrugged. "I don't really like managing, I like designing. I resigned as CEO years ago and hired one of the co-owners to manage the company. In reality, I'm not even the Chief Technical Officer, I'm more like an outside consultant."

None of that really mattered to Mia, so she turned back to the car. "So what is this prototype?" Mia asked, feeling a little bit out of her league. It was obviously a car, but other than that she wasn't sure what she was looking at.

"The best way to describe it is a sporty minivan," he explained. He moved his hand over the designs and pulled up some artist renditions of the car. It was sleek like a sports car but definitely made to hold more than the traditional five passengers.

"Is it electric like your newer models?" Mia asked, pointing to the engine.

Carter nodded. He pulled up a different screen on the drafting desk to a new set of schematics that Mia assumed were for some sort of engine. "We've increased the battery capability to extend range as well as increased torque for more power."

Mia glanced up at him, watching the way excitement lit up his face as he spoke about his car. He looked different now that he was talking about cars. He wasn't the rancher anymore, he was the car man now. She wasn't sure which one she liked better, but both versions suited him.

"It looks beautiful," she said, after a moment of looking at the model. "But, I'd never be able to afford one of your cars, so I'm not sure I'm a good person to ask about it."

"If you could afford it, would you be interested?"

"A W Motors electric car that seats seven and looks like this?" She motioned to the model. "Hell yes. But it's never going to happen. I don't even make enough to even test drive one."

Carter grinned. "The base price is going to be thirty thousand."

Mia did a double take. She had expected the price to have another zero. "What?"

"That's what's so special about this design," he explained. He looked over the designs the same way he had looked at Hopeful Dreamer- with love. "We figured out how to get the cost down. You interested?"

"Very." Mia nodded. "It's still more than I should spend, but it's possible. When will it be available?"

He took a step closer to her and changed the design schematics on the drafting table again. "Soon. Now that the airbag lawsuit is almost finished, this car can go into production. I want to give us enough time to test and make sure it's the safest car on the market."

"I heard about that lawsuit," Mia said. "Something with the airbags not deploying properly?"

Carter nodded. His smile fell, and the shadows grew on

his face. "Yes. There were injuries and several deaths due to the airbags in an older model of one of my cars."

"I'm sorry."

He shrugged, but she could still see the weight on his shoulders. It still bothered him. "We've fixed it, but I want to make sure it never happens again. I want my cars to be safe, even if it means delays."

"You really care, don't you?" Mia asked, watching his face. His brows were drawn and eyes serious.

He turned sharply to look at her, his eyebrows rising in surprise.

"I mean, billionaires are always painted as uncaring, money-hungry tycoons. But you honestly do care," she explained.

"Money-hungry?" he crossed his arms and raised an eyebrow.

Mia's cheeks heated. She hadn't thought that sentence through. She'd meant it as a compliment, but it obviously hadn't come out as one.

"Okay, not quite that bad," she revised with a bashful smile.

"I better have my publicist work on my image," he said. "I specifically requested to be seen as elitist and greedy. I'm going to have to fire all of them." He winked at her, letting her know there were no hard feelings.

Mia let out a small laugh. "You take that really well."

Carter shrugged. "I've been called many things. You get used to it after a while."

Mia's heart ached for him. He didn't deserve to be called any of those things. From what she'd seen of the man, he was the exact antithesis of greedy or uncaring. She was glad she hadn't known who he was. She would have come in with a preconceived idea of what

Carter would be like. He was rich, but he wasn't spoiled.

Carter cleared his throat and motioned to the designs. "What features would you want in a car like this?"

"Cup-holders," Mia answered immediately. "More cup-holders than seem necessary. With kids, you need as many as possible."

Carter chuckled and made a note on the drafting table, leaning over the table rather than using the chair. "Done. What else?"

Mia took a breath in as she thought. "A built-in vacuum. Smart doors that won't hit things when opened, easy to clean mats, door locks that are easy to take out of child mode... and did I mention cup-holders?"

Carter laughed. "No, I don't think you did mention those. This is why I need you."

He leaned forward and added her ideas to his list on the table. He was so close that she could smell the soft scent of his soap. It was clean and masculine without being over-powering. It made her tremble with sudden desire.

The room was suddenly warm as her thoughts went from cars to how his muscles moved under his shirt. She wondered what he looked like with his shirt off and what his skin would feel like under her fingertips. Who cared about cup-holders anyway?

As if reading her thoughts, he stopped writing and looked up at her. Slowly, he came to his full height, and as she looked up at him, he reached for her. His fingers were cool and soft as they curled around the small tendrils of hair at the base of her neck. His touch on her bare skin sent desire snaking through her spine and down to her core.

The corner of his mouth turned up in a tiny, but confident, smile, and he leaned forward to kiss her. She forgot how to breathe, but it didn't matter. This felt so right, even with her heart pounding a million miles an hour.

The kiss never happened. Their lips never connected and everything went wrong. Just as their lips were about to touch, a sharp knock came on the garage door. They both paused. The door opened and the moment was ruined.

Mia turned. If it was one of her kids asking for the millionth time for pizza for dinner, she was going to murder them.

Only it wasn't her kids. It was the giant security guard from the first day on the ranch. Somehow, he was even bigger than she remembered. Scarier.

"Is the boy in here?" the man asked, his voice as deep as he was big.

"Which boy?" Carson asked, dropping his hand from Mia's neck.

"The youngest. Laura says he's not with the others. We can't find him."

Chapter 7

$\mathcal{M}$ia

"WHAT DO YOU MEAN, 'can't find him'?" Mia asked, the blood draining out of her face.

"Laura was working with the older two, turned around, and he was gone," the security guard explained. He looked around the garage. "She thought maybe he followed the two of you here."

"You mean you don't know where Grayson is?" she clarified, needing to hear the words.

"No ma'am. We don't know where he is."

Mia's stomach dropped out, and her knees felt shaky. Luckily, Carter reached out and steadied her. If he hadn't grabbed her hand, there was a very real chance that she would have fallen over. She focused for the moment on his fingers and the strength in his grip. He was the only solid thing in the world for a moment as worry flooded through her.

"We'll find him, Mia," Carter promised. "He can't have gone far."

His promise was sweet to her ears, and she tried to nod in agreement. He still had her hand, and it helped keep the panic from clawing its way up her throat and strangling her.

"Do you know where he might have gone?" the security guard asked. His dark eyes were serious and calm. He didn't look panicked, and that made Mia feel a tiny bit better.

"No." Mia shook her head. "He wasn't excited about touching the horses since they're so big, but I don't know where he'd go... I'll check the car."

"Brian, I want the ranch on full alert," Carter said, still holding her hand. "All hands on deck."

"Yes, sir." Brian nodded curtly and grabbed the radio at his shoulder.

Mia didn't wait to hear him call it in. She let go of Carter's hand and ran to her car. She was breathless from sprinting when she got there. It was unlocked.

His school backpack was in there, but not him.

Her hands started shaking, and the world grayed out. She'd never lost one of her kids. She made sure she was always conscious of where they were. She had helped search for runaways, but no one had ever gone missing while under her care. She hated this feeling. She wanted Grayson safe in her arms.

"It's okay, Mia," Carter told her as he caught up and found her holding onto the car. "We'll find him. He has to be on the ranch somewhere."

Mia was already imagining the worst. Rattlesnakes, coyotes, bears, mountain lions, kidnappers, open wells, and rabid dogs were all running through her mind. Her heart rate was through the roof, and her whole body wound like a too-tight spring. It took everything she had not to start running around screaming his name.

"Let's check the stables again." Carter took her arm and calmly led her down the neat stone path to the stables. Mia tried to concentrate on how steadying he felt next to her instead of her own panic. Grayson had to be okay. He had to be.

"I'm so sorry," Laura told her as they walked in. Her eyes were big and full of worry. "He was just here. He didn't want to touch the horse just yet, so I let him be for a moment. He was just sitting right there on that stool, and I turned around, and..."

"It's okay, Laura," Carter said. He reached out and gave Laura's shoulder a gentle squeeze. "You keep the other two calm while we look around."

Lily and Alexander looked up from the horse they were grooming. Mia did her best to smile. They didn't realize their brother was really missing, which was good. If they knew, they would only panic too and make things worse.

"I looked everywhere," Laura whispered. "I told them he probably had to go to the bathroom."

"We'll find him," Carter told Laura. He sounded so confident that it had to be true. Mia needed to hear him say it as many times as possible. She was so glad he was staying calm and directing them because she felt like a total mess. His calmness and assured manner was the only thing keeping her from going off the deep end and completely freaking out.

"Where could he have gone?" Mia asked, looking around. The stall doors were all open with the horses out in the pasture, so she knew he wasn't in one of them. Everything was airy and open, which was nice, but it made for no good hiding places.

Carter got a thoughtful look as he glanced around. "Did you check the hayloft?"

"It was the first place I looked," Laura told him.

"Did you go up there? Or just stick your head up?" Carter asked.

"I just stuck my head up," Laura replied. Her eyes widened with hope and whatever idea Carter already had.

"Come with me, Mia," Carter said, tugging on Mia's hand. "I know where I'd go if I were a kid here."

Mia tried to take deep, steadying breaths, but her lungs weren't working right. The shallow panicky breaths were just too easy. She knew she had to calm down, or else she'd be no good in a search. In her mind, she was already making the phone call to the police, to her boss, and to Margie. What in the world was she going to say?

"This way, Mia," Carter said softly. She'd frozen in the middle of the barn. He took her hand and tugged gently. She focused on him. He was calm, and she latched onto that, needing his serenity.

Together they went to the hayloft and climbed the ladder. Mia sneezed halfway up. It was dusty and smelled like clean hay. It was a nice scent, just one she wasn't used to.

"There's nobody up here," she moaned, looking around as she followed Carter up. All she could see was piles and bales of yellow hay everywhere. Panic clawed at her throat again and twisted her stomach into knots. "What if he's hurt?"

Carter walked around a stack of hay. "He's over here," he called softly.

Mia gasped with relief as she ran over the slippery hay. Carter was kneeling next to a sleeping Grayson. He was curled up like a little barn cat on the soft hay. A small smile was on his petite features as he dreamed.

Relief was a physical sensation that washed over her. Her voice cracked as she said his name. "Grayson."

The little boy's eyes fluttered open from whatever dream he was having. Mia was on her knees hugging him to her chest.

"I was tired," he announced, pulling back slightly. Several pieces of hay were stuck in his dark hair. He yawned. "What are you guys doing up here?"

Mia hugged Grayson close, ignoring his protests. Tears were streaming down her cheeks, and she knew it was going to turn into an ugly cry at any moment, but she didn't care. "You scared us," she whispered.

Grayson looked up at her confused. "I was just resting. It's quiet up here."

Carter ruffled the boy's hair. "Next time, let someone know before you come up here. Okay?"

Grayson nodded, his eyes still full of sleep. As far as he knew, he'd just found a comfy spot and the adults had rudely woken him up. He looked back and forth between Mia and Carter like they were both crazy.

"I'll go tell Brian to call off the search," Carter said, rising to his feet.

Mia grabbed at his pant leg. "Thank you so much, Carter."

He smiled and gently squeezed her shoulder before heading back down the loft ladder. Mia hugged Grayson to her again, sniffling as she held him tight.

"You okay, Mia?" Grayson asked. He let her hold him but clearly didn't understand what all the fuss was about.

Mia wiped her face. "Yeah. You just really scared me. I didn't know where you were."

Grayson's eyes got big as he realized that she had thought he was missing or had run away. "Am I in trouble?"

"No, not this time." Mia shook her head and gave him another hug. "Just don't ever do that again. Tell somebody where you're going. Always."

"Yes, Mia." He tucked his chin into her shoulder and snuggled into her. "I'm sorry I scared you. I'll never do it again."

"I'm just glad you are okay." Mia let out a shaky sigh and hugged him to her as she waited for her heartbeat to slow down. It took a couple of minutes before she was ready to let him go. "Let's go back down. I'm sure your brother and sister will want to see you."

He gave her one more hug before standing up and brushing the hay from his shirt. Together they climbed the ladder back down to the stables.

Carter was in the stall with the other two children, helping them groom one of the horses. Mia didn't recognize this horse, so it wasn't Hopeful Dreamer.

"And that's all you have to do," Carter explained, showing them something with the brush. Both of the older kids were listening to him with rapt attention. He smiled as Mia and Grayson came into view. "Here they are. See? Safe and sound."

Lily and Alexander's shoulders relaxed. Even though they didn't know just how missing their brother had been, they had been worried. Lily pulled her little brother into her for a quick hug before picking a piece of hay from his hair.

"You want to touch the horse?" Lily asked her youngest brother. "This one is nice."

Grayson looked apprehensively back and forth between his sister and the big animal.

"You don't have to if you don't want to," Mia told him. The last thing she needed was more drama today.

"What if I show you the secret trick to make horses love you?" Carter asked. He dropped down to a squat, so he was the same height as Grayson. "That way, you'll always know what to do."

Grayson smiled shyly at Carter and nodded. Carter patted him on the shoulder as he rose and went to the far end of the stable to retrieve something. He came back with an apple.

"This horse's name is Heartbreaker," Carter told him. He pulled out a pocket knife and efficiently cut the apple into slices. "Hold out your hand."

Grayson timidly held out his small hand for Carter to place an apple slice. Carter then moved behind the boy and helped support Grayson's hand with his own.

"Hold your hand out with the apple flat in your palm," Carter instructed. "Keep your fingers straight so that she won't accidentally catch them. There you go."

Mia held her breath as the horse daintily took the apple slice from Grayson. Grayson's face went from one of uncertainty to one of joy as the horse munched happily.

"It tickles," Grayson said with a giggle.

Carter gave the boy a gentle squeeze before letting him go to stand up. "Now she knows that you're her friend and that you give apples. She'll always be nice to you."

Grayson reached out a tentative hand to pet the horse's strong neck. Heartbreaker simply chewed on her apple slice. Grayson grinned and gained confidence, petting her more enthusiastically each time.

"She's not so scary now," he said.

Carter chuckled and put his hands on Grayson's shoulders. It was such a pretty picture that Mia wished she had a camera. It could have been staged for a publicity shoot to improve Carter's image for how perfect it was. It made her heart happy because it was real.

Grayson let out a huge yawn that cracked his jaws and made Mia check her watch.

"It's time to go," she said, hating that she was the one ending the day.

A chorus of disappointed childrens' grumbles followed her announcement.

"We'll be back tomorrow," Mia promised. "But we have to get you home for dinner."

The older children put away the grooming supplies without too much more whining. Mia helped, but she watched Carter and Grayson from the corner of her eye as she stacked brushes and cloths.

"You did well with the horse today." Carter knelt before Grayson with a hand on his shoulder. "No more scaring Mia and I'll teach you how to ride a horse. Deal?"

Grayson's face split into a giant grin as he looked up at the horse and then back to Carter. "Deal!"

Mia smiled, her heart suddenly lighter than she remembered it ever being. His biography said he didn't want children, but he sure was a natural with them.

"Come on, guys," Mia called, leaving the barn and heading to the car. Three kids and Carter followed reluctantly. "Make sure to buckle up."

Lily helped Grayson with his booster seat buckle since it seemed to always stick while Alexander got himself settled.

"Thank you, Carter," Mia said, coming around to the side of the car next to him. The words didn't seem like enough.

"Anytime," he replied, watching the kids in the car.

Mia paused for a moment, but then hugged him. He

froze at her sudden gesture, but then wrapped his arms around her and returned the hug. His arms felt safe and strong wrapped around her. It wasn't the same as the almost kiss in the garage, but there was definitely something between them. It was a short embrace, with Mia pulling back before she could embarrass herself. He smelled so good, like hay and sunshine, that there was a very real risk of her not ever letting go.

Chapter 8

arter

F<small>IRE ENGULFED THE PARKING GARAGE</small>, *a demon of red and orange that relentlessly pursued him. The heat of the flames licked at his skin and singed his eyebrows. His lungs struggled for oxygen as the fire stole it with every desperate inhale.*

Carter coughed and tried to run from the fire, but his feet were stuck to the ground. He forced his legs to move, but every step was like through quicksand. His eyes watered with the acrid smoke of burning plastic and metal. Sweat drenched his body as he struggled to get away.

Somehow the flames grew. Carter panicked, his feet turning to stone as the flames consumed him.

And then he woke up.

～

C<small>ARTER SAT STRAIGHT</small> up in bed, gasping for air and clawing at his bed-sheets. It was just a nightmare. It was the nightmare he'd had every night since the incident.

He sucked in the clean mountain air, trying to convince his lungs that he wasn't still trapped in the smoke and fire of the dream. His heart rate was through the roof, and he was going to need to change the sheets on the bed. They were soaked with sweat.

He heaved himself out of the covers and out of bed, reveling in the feel of the cold tile on his feet as he made his way to the bathroom and splashed some water on his face. The man in the mirror looked haggard and exhausted, but not burned. His eyebrows were intact, and there wasn't soot in his hair.

It helped convince him it had been just a dream.

Still, there was no way Carter was going back to sleep after that. When he closed his eyes, the flames came back, though less vibrant with every minute he was awake. Regardless, he wasn't about to risk falling into the dream again. He'd rather go to the garage and work than risk the dream again.

He threw on a pair of well-loved jeans, finding a hole in the knee. He frowned at it, then shrugged. It didn't matter what he looked like here, so he could just be comfortable. He put a clean t-shirt on and a pair of slip-on shoes to walk the short distance to the garage.

"It was just a dream," he whispered to himself as he went down the stairs. "It isn't real. It didn't happen again."

He shivered. The flames had been so real. It had felt the same as that day when he nearly died a month ago. He'd come to the ranch to escape those flames, but still, they chased him through his dreams.

Outside the stars twinkled and shone. The breeze was cold, but Carter didn't bother grabbing a jacket. It was just a short walk, and the garage would be warm enough. He hurried across the gravel path, noticing at least one security guard watching him.

The garage was quiet and serene. He took a deep breath in, smelling motor oil and metal. It was soothing and comforting. Here, the dream couldn't get him. He was safe here.

He went to his drafting table and turned it on. He lazily pulled up some design ideas and started playing around with future model ideas for his cars. Most of them would never be put into production, but he enjoyed the process of creation.

A yawn cracked his jaws, and he glanced at the clock. It was just after one in the morning. He really should go back to bed, but he hesitated. He didn't want the dream again, so instead, he forced himself to remember.

It had been a long day at work. There was always so much to do when preparing a beta for a new design. The test model was coming along nicely, and he was excited to see how it held up to testing in the next couple of weeks. He was ready to head home, take a long shower, and go to bed early.

He waved goodnight to his secretary and headed out to the parking garage. Keys in hand, he walked to his designated spot near the door. Any other day, he would have gone straight to the driver's seat and started the engine, but today, he forgot his phone on his desk.

He sighed and thought about just leaving it for the night, but decided against it. He had to go back inside for it.

He was close enough for the car to recognize his key fob and begin to uncurl the mirrors and turn on the engine. He pushed a button on his keys to remote start his car so it would be cool by the time he returned. Since it was electric, he didn't have to worry about wasting gas. He'd just go grab his phone and be on his way to bed before he knew it.

He didn't see the explosion. He was halfway through the door when the bomb under his car went off. Turning on the car had triggered it. The heavy door leading out of the garage took most of the impact. Still, the noise deafened him, and the smoke blistered his eyes. Flames and car parts rained down inside the parking garage. Fire filled his vision.

∾

THE POLICE SAID he was lucky. If he'd been inside the car when he started it, he would have been dead. He couldn't decide if the remote start or forgetting his phone had saved his life. Either way, he was making remote starts standard on all his cars from now on.

Suddenly, the death threats to his office had taken a new meaning. The police had almost no leads to work with. All the pieces of the bomb could be bought at a regular gas station, and the security cameras were disabled at the time of the blast. All they had to work with was that someone wanted Carter Williamson dead.

Unfortunately, given the amount of people who sent him death threats because they felt wronged by his cars, the list was rather long.

They'd whisked him away to Stone Mountain Ranch in Colorado and told everyone who didn't need to know that he was at his ranch in Tennessee for a vacation.

No one except his security team and his main assistant knew he was here. He was safe from car bombs here, other than in dreams. He had cameras and security personnel making sure no one got within a quarter mile of him without consent. He was here to make sure that the death threats stayed threats rather than reality. Once the police caught the person responsible, he could go back to his regular life in the city, but until then, he was trapped on the ranch. He loved the ranch, but he couldn't leave which frustrated him.

Carter scrubbed his face, feeling the prickles of a beard forming on his chin. He'd need to shave before Mia and the kids arrived. The thought of Mia drove the flames from his mind and he smiled for the first time since waking up.

She made being out on the ranch more fun than he'd expected. Her visits and the smiles of the kids were the highlights of his day and he found himself wishing they were at the ranch more often. He felt better when they were there. Less alone.

In his mind's eye, he saw her smile. Her pixie nose and crinkled eyes made his heart lighter and he let a yawn overtake him. She was a dream he would happily take. He yawned again and switched off the drafting table. Bed, with dreams of Mia, suddenly sounded like something he could handle. She would keep the dreams of flame at bay.

CARTER HAD to resist the urge to throw the piece of paper wrapped in a plastic bag as hard as he could. He wanted to rip it to shreds, but it was evidence and needed to be saved. Instead of chucking it, he handed it back to his head of security.

"You'll pay. It's your fault she's dead. You're next" The words glared up at him from a plain sheet of white paper.

"And you can't find anything on it?" Carter asked,

looking at it the way most people would look at a venomous snake. For a moment, flames danced across his vision, but he pushed them away. This was just a piece of paper. Nothing more.

Brian shook his head. "No leads. It's from a generic printer on generic paper. The return address is a cheap motel in Texas. We're checking it out, but it doesn't look like it's going to tell us who sent this."

Carter turned from Brian and looked out the window at the mountains. People died in car crashes all the time, so since he made cars, people often blamed him. He understood that. He could commiserate with many of them, and as such, he rarely took the threats sent to his business personally.

This letter unsettled him. He was used to getting threats of all kinds at his office in the city. Or, rather he had been until a couple of weeks ago, but getting one here was a different matter.

He wasn't supposed to receive them here. No one was even supposed to know he was at the ranch, let alone even in Colorado. The address wasn't even publicly listed, and the one on record went to a PO box just outside of town. He'd even gotten his address removed from the Internet map programs. There was no way for a threat to be delivered here.

Except one had been. This threat was on his doorstep, waiting for him. They knew where he was. This was personal. This had to be related to the bomb. They still hadn't caught the person who had tried to kill him. Unease ate his belly. But, he wasn't going to run again. This was the still the safest place for him.

Carter watched as a cloud danced across the tip of the mountain, changing the play of the shadows. Whoever sent this was close. They were watching him. They knew he was here and how to get to him.

This letter wasn't just a threat. It was a warning that whoever had sent it knew exactly what they were doing.

It was unnerving, to say the least.

"And nothing new on the security front? Nothing happened?" Carter turned from the window and back to Brian.

"No, sir. It's quiet, just like it always is. I even went over the security footage, and whoever it was stayed in the cameras' blind spots. I didn't even know there was one, but all we have of the guy is that he's wearing jeans."

"Like every other person in the state," Carter replied. He could feel a headache starting to form.

"But, with the arrival of this letter, I've stepped up patrols." Brian stood up straighter. "Do you want me to hire more men? I added three guys to the roster a week ago, but I can find more."

Carter shook his head. More bodies weren't the solution to this.

"No." He frowned. "Are you sure about the new guys?"

"They all passed the background screens, and you know how thorough I am," Brian explained. "Everyone came highly recommended. I don't think they had anything to do with the letter or getting it here."

He trusted Brian with his life. If Brian said the new guys were good, then they were. Carter nodded. "Good."

"Do you want me to cancel with Ms. Amesworth?" Brian asked. "The children don't need to come this afternoon."

"No!" Carter said too quickly. Seeing Mia and the kids was the only thing he was looking forward to today. He'd been looking forward to it since waking up last night. "No. I promised them we'd go riding today. As long as there isn't an imminent threat, I want them here."

"Of course, sir," Brian deferred. He paused for a moment, then smiled, his stern features softening slightly as he thought about the kids. He obviously had a soft spot for them as much as Carter did. "The work has been good for those kids. They'll enjoy the ride today."

"Yes, they will," he agreed. A small smile crossed Carter's face.

But, he wasn't smiling about how much the kids would like it. He was thinking about how good it was going to be to see Mia.

Chapter 9

*M*ia

MIA APPRAISED the brown quarter horse in front of her, not quite entirely sure how confident she felt getting back up on the horse by herself. The gelding looked steady enough, but it had been a long time since Mia had been on a horse. She remembered it being fun, but she didn't remember the horses looking quite so big. She decided to wait a moment before getting on. The kids would probably need her help.

"Why do I have to wear a helmet?" Alexander asked, looking askance at the riding helmet they all had to wear. He held it in front of him like it smelled as he waited to get up on his horse. "Cowboys wear hats."

"You wear it because I like your head in one piece," Mia told him. "And you need more practice to be a cowboy."

Alexander opened his mouth to complain, but Carter held up a helmet of his own.

"I'm wearing a helmet," Carter informed him, putting

the heavy helmet on his own head. He shrugged like it was nothing. "These don't blow off in the wind, so I actually like it better than a hat."

Mia could have kissed him for the little white lie. Alexander stopped pouting and immediately put his helmet on without a fuss. Carter gave her a wink as he walked over to her.

"Here," Carter said, coming up beside her and handing her a sugar cube. "For your horse. His name's Jasper."

He stood next to her in the arena as they got the kids ready for their first ride. The touch of his hand sent flutters through her stomach and she couldn't have stopped the smile that filled her face if she'd tried.

"Thank you for the helmet help," Mia said quietly. She held out her hand and gave it to her horse, holding her hand out flat.

"For that?" Carter replied. He knocked the helmet with his knuckles loudly. "I really do like this better."

She laughed at his easy manner as he walked away. She shook her head and reached down to tighten the straps to her saddle and fix the stirrups. She'd had lessons for a few months when she was Alexander's age. It was right after she'd been put in the foster care system and was one of the few good memories she had. She'd always been drawn to horses since that.

Mia's horse was tied to the arena fence along with the kids' horses. Lily was in the process of getting up on a gentle looking light gray mare.

"You're a natural," Laura told Lily, as Lily settled into the saddle. The teenager looked more comfortable up on the horse than she did on the ground. Lily grinned as Laura moved to help her brother up onto his horse.

Alexander had a determined look in his eye as he used

the mounting block to get up on his own brown gelding. Once there, he grinned proudly and let out a loud, "Yee-haw!"

"You're up next, Grayson," Laura told him as she fixed the stirrups to better fit Alexander's long legs.

Grayson had the apprehensive look again from the other day. He kept looking up at his horse like she might step on him. Mia patted her horse and started to go to him, but Carter beat her there.

"You ready?" Carter asked, kneeling in front to the boy. He took Grayson's small hand in his and walked the boy over to the horse that he was going to ride. She was the smallest horse there, more of a pony than a horse, but Mia could see how Grayson might still feel intimidated by her size. Her dark gray features were kind and friendly.

"I don't know," Grayson replied slowly. He stopped short of touching the horse. "She's awfully big."

Carter handed him a sugar cube and leaned over to whisper in Grayson's ear.

"Don't tell the others, but she's my favorite," he told the boy. "There's a reason she's named Sweetness."

Grayson held out the sugar cube, giggling as the horse daintily took it from him. She crunched it happily as she let him pet her. Grayson ran his small hand along her gray coat, watching her eat the sugar and steeling his nerve.

"Will you help me up?" Grayson finally asked, looking up at Carter.

In one smooth motion, Carter had him up in the saddle. Grayson laughed with delight.

"Now, use your legs to hold on to her," Carter advised, patting Grayson's legs. "It's all about your legs. The reins are for steering, but even if you drop them, she'll listen to what you tell her to do with your legs."

Grayson nodded nervously. He had the reins in one hand and the saddle pommel in the other, and a death grip on both, but he was smiling. Mia's heart swelled with pride at his bravery. This was hard for him and he was doing a good job.

Carter slowly led him around the arena, giving him pointers on what to do with his legs and his hands. Laura had Lily and Alexander who were already getting their horses to walk, stop and turn around the arena without help.

Mia turned to see Grayson laugh as Carter started to jog with the horse leads. Sweetness was living up to her name, giving as gentle a ride as she could. Grayson's fear had evaporated.

"You're doing great," Carter told Grayson as he slowed to a stop next to Laura. Laura guided the pony over behind the other two children. Laura would lead the ride, with Lily and Alexander behind her, then Grayson, then Mia, and followed up in the rear by Carter.

Mia turned back to her horse. Now that the children were ready, it was time to mount up and get going.

"You ready?" Carter asked, coming up beside her. He wasn't even winded from jogging with Grayson.

"I was born ready," Mia informed him. She put her foot in the stirrup and confidently swung herself up on the horse. She remembered it being a lot harder when she was little, but that was probably due to her size. She went up smoothly and settled into the saddle like an old pro.

Carter raised an impressed eyebrow and pride warmed Mia's chest. She kept her head up, sending a huge thank you for the childhood lessons, and nudged her horse to join the kids. She let out a small sigh of relief when the horse did exactly as she asked. The last thing she wanted was to look foolish in front of Carter. She rather liked that impressed look on him.

"Okay, we ready to go?" Laura asked from her own horse. When everyone nodded, she moved to the front of the line. "Then I think we're ready for our ride."

Alexander let out a loud whoop that made Mia wince, but none of the horses even flicked an ear. It made Mia less anxious about their ride. These horses were steady and calm.

Laura led the line of horses out to a path alongside one of the paddocks. It was a perfect early September day. The sky was so blue that it hurt Mia's eyes to look at it for too long. The aspens were still green, but the grass was starting to yellow. Mia was glad she'd worn a light jacket. The breeze coming down the mountains and across the big open meadow was cool and fresh.

The horses walked at a comfortable, sedate pace that was perfect for the children. All three of them had smiles on their faces and were having a fantastic time. Alexander kept talking with what she assumed was a cowboy accent. He kept calling everyone "y'all" and "pardner" but the rest of the accent sounded more like he was having a stroke than a drawl.

Mia took a deep breath of clean air into her lungs. This was a little piece of heaven. The horse moved smoothly under her. She could feel the gelding's power, but it was contained and calm. It was incredibly zen and Mia slowed her breathing to match the horse's strides. Her legs were going to be sore tomorrow, but today, it was worth it.

"Having fun?" Carter asked, coming up beside her.

She grinned. "The best. Thank you."

"You look like you never left the saddle," he commented. She felt a blush of pride cross her cheeks.

"I bet you say that to all the girls you take out on horseback," she replied.

He thought for a moment and then nodded. "You're right, I do." She looked over at him surprised that he would admit such a thing and he grinned. "Because you're the only girl I've ever taken out on horseback."

It was a good thing that her horse was doing the walking, or she would have stopped in the middle of the path. He kept on riding like it was nothing, but she felt incredibly special.

"Really?" she asked, urging her horse to go a little bit faster to ride next to him. "You've never taken a girl out here?"

"I guess if you want to be technical, I have come out here with Laura," he replied. "But, since she's an employee, and I think of her like my little sister, then I don't think it really counts."

"So, I'm special?" she asked. Her cheeks heated as soon as she realized she'd said the words out loud.

He turned, focusing the full power of his blue eyes on her. When he looked at her, it was as if there were nothing else in the world. He made her feel like the center of everything. It was a heady experience that left her a little breathless.

"Yes." He said it like a simple truth and her insides went to mush.

"Thank you," she whispered. He nodded, not releasing her from his gaze. She cleared her throat, her heart fluttering in her chest with his direct gaze. "So, do you come out here with Laura often?"

The corners of his mouth twitched up in a smile. "Jealous?"

"Maybe a little," she admitted, and he laughed.

"We go out about once a week when I'm here in Silver Springs," he told her. He glanced up at where Laura was explaining something about riding to Lily. "When I first bought this place, I hired Laura to run it. She had amazing recommendations. I went riding with her and they were all well-deserved. I'd owned this place for two years but only came to visit a handful of times. No one really knows that it's mine."

His horse walked calmly next to Mia's, the two horses in sync as their riders talked. In front of them, the kids enjoyed their horseback ride.

"There's some local gossip that a billionaire bought this place, but no one knew which one. Most people think it's going to be turned into houses at some point," Mia replied.

"I have no plans to do that," he assured her. "I like this place as it is. It's too wild and beautiful to be a block of homes."

"Do you plan on staying here?" Mia asked. Her throat tightened at the last word, surprising her with how much she hoped the answer was a long time. She wanted him to stay forever.

"I'm not sure," he said after a moment. "I didn't expect to be here this long, to be honest."

"Oh." Mia's face fell and she looked off toward the mountains so he wouldn't see.

"It's not that I don't want to be here," he said quickly. "It's just that my business is back in California."

"So why are you here then?" Mia asked.

"It's complicated," Carter replied. He sighed. "I'm hiding out here. No one knows that I'm at this ranch, or even in the state."

"Why?" Mia turned to look at him.

"There have been some threats," he said, his voice emotionless.

Mia's eyes widened. "Oh my god! Why would someone want to hurt you?"

"That's what I'd like to know." His expression was grim and his eyes distant. For a moment, he looked much older and worn than he really was, but then he shook himself and smiled at her, bringing back the light to his eyes. "It's nothing to worry about," he promised. "It's more precautionary than anything. Please, forget I said anything."

Mia suspected there was more to it than that, but she didn't want to pry. She tried to remember if the internet had said anything about him being in danger, but nothing came to mind. "If you need anything, let me know," she offered. "Even if it's just someone to talk to."

His eyes softened as he looked at her and he smiled. "Thank you."

"I mean it," she said. "Anytime."

The horses caused their legs to bump into each other. He reached out and touched her leg, sending electricity straight to her brain. How was it that he had this effect on her? Just a casual touch had her body aching for more of him. She found herself hoping he'd take her up on her offer.

The horses moved apart as the path widened again. She missed his touch already.

"So, are you seeing anyone?" he asked. Mia nearly fell off her horse.

"No, I mean... the kids... I..." She regained her poise and cleared her throat. "No, I'm not."

Carter chuckled, obviously enjoying that he caught her off guard.

"What about you?" she asked, her heart starting to pound in her chest. He probably had half a dozen swimsuit models on speed dial, so she was trying very hard not to get her hopes up. Not that she even had a chance with him, anyway.

"Not currently," he replied. He glanced over at her. "But that could change."

Mia's heart went into overdrive. "Is that so?"

He grinned at her and she suddenly understood how women could swoon at the sight of a man. If she'd been standing, the force of that smile would have made her knees buckle. She was just glad she didn't fall off the horse.

The man was dangerous with that smile.

Mia decided to take control of herself.

"So I told you all about myself the other day," she said. "But, what about you? Tell me about yourself."

"I'm sure you've read my biography online," he replied. "What else do you want to know?"

"I only skimmed it," she told him. "And it didn't have your favorite food. Or color. Or what you like to do on a Saturday night."

He chuckled. "Pizza, blue, and, you can't tell anyone this, but on Saturdays, I put on a special suit and fight crime."

"You're Batman?" Mia made sure to put enough awe into her voice and widen her eyes like she was surprised.

"I'm Batman," Carter said, his voice going low and gravely. Mia couldn't help but giggle. Carter shrugged. "It's expected of billionaires these days to be a superhero. If you don't fight crime, you lose status."

"That actually makes a lot of sense," Mia replied, nodding. "Who is Bill Gates, then?"

"I don't reveal other superheroes' identities," Carter told her. Then he glanced around as if someone might be watching before leaning over to whisper. "He's actually

Superman. How do you think he came up with the idea for his computers? They're from his home-world."

"Things make so much more sense," Mia said. "I've always wondered about that. How is it being a superhero?"

"Pretty awesome actually," Carter told her. He grinned at her. "You want to see my gadgets? I have a big Batarang."

"That sounds almost dirty," Mia replied, giving him the side-eye.

"Only to dirty minds." He waggled his eyebrows at her and winked.

Mia laughed. "Where do you keep it? In the garage? Under the barn? Where is your Bat-cave?"

"If I told you, I'd have to kill you," Carter replied, shrugging his shoulders as he guided his horse along the path.

"Wait, Batman doesn't kill people. It's one of his things," Mia said.

"That's why I can't tell you," Carter explained. "If I don't tell you, then I don't have to kill you."

"That makes perfect sense," Mia said, nodding and chuckling. "If you're a superhero, who are the super villains? Other billionaires?"

"No, not other billionaires." He leaned over again to whisper. "The bad guys are actually just millionaires. That's why it's so easy for us to defeat them. And why there's so many more bad guys than good guys."

Mia chuckled. "I guess that's where the expression, 'crime doesn't pay' comes from. Since millionaires keep losing to billionaires."

Carter laughed, the sound going all the way into the mountains with his joy. Mia loved it and felt the warmth of pride from making him laugh fill her. She wished she had the power to make him laugh like that all the time.

"So, I've always wondered, how do you order all the

gadgets without anyone suspecting?" Mia asked. "I mean, I buy one thing online and suddenly I have ads all for everything related. How do you not have Amazon know what you're buying?"

"The guy who owns Amazon is a billionaire too, you know," Carter explained. "He has his own secret superhero identity and thus makes sure that we all get to preserve ours. It's a group effort."

"I guess that means you know all the other heroes," Mia said. "I've always wanted to meet Green Arrow. What's he like?"

"Boring," Carter said quickly. "He's totally and completely boring and you don't ever want to meet him. Batman is way better. And stronger. And better looking."

"Is that so?" Mia pretended to think for a minute before smiling at him. "Batman always was my favorite."

"Good." Carter grinned at her. "So, you want to see my Batarang?" He waggled his eyebrows and glanced down toward his saddle with a naughty wink.

Mia nearly fell off her horse laughing.

Chapter 10

M ia

LAURA LED the line of horses up a path away from the ranch. They were still in the foothills, but it was close enough to a mountain ride to feel on top of the world. Wildflowers, pine trees, and panoramic views for as far as she could see surrounded her. The scent of pine and dry grass warmed by the sunshine filled her nose. Peaceful was the best word Mia could think of to describe the beauty of the mountains.

Mia and Carter talked and laughed as they rode their horses. They stayed slightly back behind the kids, enjoying their private conversation. Mia couldn't remember the last time she'd laughed this hard. Carter kept cracking jokes and flirting with her the entire ride up into the foothills. This was the best day she'd had in a long time.

After about an hour, the path opened to a small meadow. The yellowing grass waved gently in the cool breeze with the mountains capped in snow behind in the distance.

"Who wants to go a little faster?" Laura asked the kids as Mia and Carter caught up with them. "This field is safe for us to run the horses in."

"I do!" Lily shouted, urging her horse closer to Laura.

"I figured you would," Laura said with a chuckle. She moved her horse so that she was next to Lily. "Use your legs and match the horse's rhythm as she goes up and down. Keep your hands low. You can rest them on the horse's neck if you want."

"Okay," Lily replied, mimicking Laura's movements. "I can do that."

Laura grinned. "Start with a canter, then lean forward. Use both your legs to ask the horse to go faster- not the reins," Laura instructed. "When you want to stop, steady the pace with your reins and sit back into the saddle. No jerky movements."

"But that's what they do in the movies," Alexander said, pretending to pull back on his reins. His horse looked back at him like he was crazy, but didn't react to him pulling on the reins.

"Movies aren't real life," Laura reminded him. "Be gentle with the reins. Would you like someone pulling hard on your mouth?"

Alexander thought about it for a moment and then relaxed his grip. He leaned forward and whispered an apology to his horse.

"Ready Lily?" Laura asked.

The grin on Lily's face was huge. She looked ready to fly with joy. The girl was so excited she could barely contain the excited nod. It made Mia's heart surge. Lily's life was all about taking care of her siblings and surviving. She deserved some fun in her life. All kids did, but especially kids like her with the weight of the world on their shoulders.

Lily followed Laura's instructions to the letter. She looked like a professional rider to Mia's eyes as she urged her horse faster and faster. The sweet mare did what she was asked, even going to a gallop for a short time before slowing. The boys cheered their sister on.

Lily's cheeks were flushed and she grinned wildly as she returned. She was on cloud nine and Mia had a feeling this was the happiest moment of her young life. Mia wished she could give this experience to all of her kids.

"Good job," Laura told her. "Anyone else want to try?"

"My turn! My turn!" Alexander chanted, urging his horse up to where Laura was.

"Okay. Show me how you hold yourself," Laura said, making sure he knew what he was doing. When she decided he was ready, she rode alongside him, encouraging him and reminding him what he needed to do. Mia held her breath as Alexander took off, but Laura was right with him.

"We went so fast!" Alexander announced, breathless and grinning when they came back. "Did you see me, Mia? Did I look like a cowboy?"

"You sure did," Mia told him. She was grinning at his excitement. When those horses ran, they were free from their pasts and their worries. If she had a million dollars, she'd have kids do this all the time.

"What about you, Grayson?" Laura asked, coming alongside the youngest kid. "Would you like to go faster?"

Grayson bit his lip and shifted his weight. He looked down at his horse and shrunk slightly. "Um..."

"You don't have to go as fast as Lily did," Laura told him.

"You can trot, which is like walking only bouncier. It's a lot of fun."

Grayson chewed on his lip for a second and then lifted his chin. "Okay," he said with a brave nod.

He sat up straight in his saddle, his head lifted and shoulders back. Slowly, his little horse gained speed with Laura right beside him. As the horse increased speed, Grayson started to grin. He lost the trepidation and urged his horse to get ahead of Laura.

"What about you?" Carter asked, coming next to Mia. His leg grazed hers as their horses found a comfortable position to stand. Her heart involuntarily sped up.

"Me?" Mia asked, looking over at him and squinting in the sunshine.

"Yeah, you." He chuckled and motioned his head toward the field. "You ready to go a little faster?"

The way he said it made her heart thud in her ears. He couldn't possibly have a second meaning, could he? Of course not. She pushed the idea out of her mind.

"I'd love to," she replied. She meant it both ways, just in case.

"I'll stay right with you," Carter said. He clucked to his horse and moved out into the field. She followed him out onto a nice dirt path that was perfect for the horses to up their speed safely. It was smooth and hole free, reminding Mia of a racetrack rather than a path. Considering Carter's wealth, she wouldn't have been surprised to find out he'd had this path made just for running his horses safely.

She kicked her heels into the muscled sides of the horse and urged him to increase his speed. The bounce and the rhythm took a second to get used to, but she loved the way it felt. Carter was right beside her, his own gelding keeping steady alongside her.

She laughed and kicked again, up to a canter. Her body naturally matched her horse, falling back on those lessons from so long ago. The wind streamed through her hair and she glanced over at Carter. Without giving him warning, she kicked again, telling the horse to stretch his legs and run.

Jasper was ready. He extended his legs out as far as he could while she leaned forward, keeping her center of gravity down on the horse like a jockey.

Carter let out a surprised sound but quickly urged his horse to match hers. Together, their horses raced along the dirt path. Each horse wanted to win the imaginary race to an imaginary finish line, so they kept pace with one another until the dirt path came to an end.

The horses came to a stop, each of them breathing hard. Mia laughed, feeling free and light. When she was on horseback, nothing could touch her. There was no problem she couldn't outrun. There was nothing but freedom.

"You're a natural," Carter told her as they turned their horses around to head back to where the kids were waiting. They went at a gentle trot now, letting their horses recover from the sprint.

"I haven't done that since I was a kid," Mia breathlessly told him. She was grinning like an idiot.

"Didn't look like it," Carter remarked. He smiled at her as they rejoined their group and she felt her cheeks heat with the compliment.

"I want to do that!" Alexander shouted. He looked ready to take off.

"Next time," Laura told him. "You still need to work on the trot and canter."

Alexander looked sly. "So, that means there's a next time?"

Laura laughed. "If you're good."

Alexander whooped. Lily grinned, and even little Grayson looked pleased with the idea of going riding again. To be honest, Mia wanted to do this again. This was a perfect day. The weather was good, the kids were happy, and the company was amazing.

She looked over at Carter. He looked so confident up on his horse. It looked like he belonged there, as much as he looked like he belonged in that garage. Both versions of him were incredibly attractive.

He caught her looking at him and grinned. She blushed hard and turned her horse back in the direction of home. The last thing she needed was for the billionaire to know she had a crush on him. She could only imagine the way he'd smile at her if he knew how much she liked him.

Laura was in the lead once more, leading the parade back to the barn. Alexander and Lily were animated up front, talking about how they wanted to practice their riding so they could gallop like Mia and Carter did. Laura was giving them pointers and promising to help.

Mia didn't see what spooked Grayson's horse. All she saw was the small gray mare suddenly shy at something on the ground and then take off running.

Time slowed, and Mia saw every blade of grass, every fiber of the horse blanket, and every hair on Grayson's head as the horse panicked and took off at a gallop through the field. It happened in the blink of an eye.

"Grayson!" Mia screamed, urging her horse to go after him. Her horse refused to budge. She had no idea what she was going to do, but Grayson was in big trouble. The horse was flying across the meadow and he was barely hanging on, his hands tangled in the mane and his little legs gripping on tight.

Carter was three steps ahead of her. He knew what to do

and had his horse ready to go. Using his larger horse's speed, he easily caught up to Grayson's panicked mare. He was able to use his own horse to slow down the terrified mare and finally bring her to a stop.

"Grayson!" Mia finally got her horse to stop being afraid of whatever he saw in the grass and she galloped him over to where Grayson was. His poor little face was sheet white and his eyes the size of dinner plates. Carter helped him unclench his hands from the mane and slide down onto the hard ground where his knees promptly gave out.

Mia was off her horse and hugging the boy as fast as she could move. Grayson shook like a leaf in her arms. The mare was frothing at the mouth, so Carter took her and walked her. He spoke low, soothing words as he let Mia take care of Grayson.

"Are you okay?" Mia asked, her hands checking him for any sign of injury. He had managed to stay on the mare the entire time, so it only looked like he was just terrified rather than hurt.

"I don't wanna ride anymore," he whispered, burying his head into her shoulder. He started to cry, the shock of what happened finally hitting him. Mia just held him and rocked back and forth.

When his breathing finally came back to normal, he sat up and wiped his eyes. His little face was blotchy and his eyes swollen with tears.

"I want to go home," Grayson whimpered. His hands held onto her shirt like the ground might take off running like the mare did and Mia was the only solid thing in his world.

"Okay," Mia told him. She wiped the tears from his cheeks and helped him stand up.

Home was a long way away. They'd ridden the horses

quite a distance, but if Grayson wanted, she was ready to walk them all the way home, even if it took until dark. She looked out at the long path back and chewed on her lip.

"How about you ride with me for a bit?" Carter asked, coming up beside them guiding the horses with him. He'd tied Grayson's mare to walk behind his horse. The mare looked exhausted and somehow embarrassed as well. "It's a long walk otherwise. Do you think you're safe with me?"

Grayson looked up at him and nodded. "You saved me."

Carter smiled and squeezed his shoulder. "I'll get up first, and then Mia will help you up. You'll sit in front of me."

Carter swung up into his saddle in a smooth motion and then made sure there was space for Grayson. With Carter's help, Mia lifted Grayson up and helped settle him in Carter's protective arms. Carter looked at ease, but Mia could see in his eyes that he wasn't going to let anything happen to that boy. She'd never seen someone look so determined and protective at the same time.

"You comfortable?" Carter asked Grayson. Grayson made sure that Carter's arms were tucked firmly around him before he nodded. He looked far less afraid with Carter holding him in place.

Carter nudged his horse into a slow walk. Grayson gripped the saddle pommel with one hand and Carter's arm with the other. The worry crept back into his face.

"You doing okay, Grayson?" Mia asked, walking alongside them with her hand on Grayson's leg. Carter led his horse in the direction of Mia's gelding.

"Carter will keep us safe, right Carter?" Grayson turned to look back at Carter.

"Super safe," Carter promised. He gave Grayson a small hug. "Nothing will happen. I promise."

Grayson nodded and gave Mia a weak grin.

"You did great, Grayson," Carter told him. "I'm really impressed. The first time that happened to me, I fell off in an instant. I landed in a bush."

"A bush?" Grayson turned to look at him.

Carter nodded. "A prickle bush. I was pulling prickles out of my hair for weeks." He pretended to pull something out of his hair while making a goofy face. Grayson giggled.

"You should get your horse, Mia." Carter nodded toward her gelding. "I've got him."

Mia gave Grayson's leg a gentle squeeze, not wanting to let go of her kid just yet. But, if they were to get home, she needed to be mounted as well. It took two tries to get up in the saddle this time, and her face was blazing as she finally settled herself.

Carter didn't say a word about it as they walked their two horses back to where Laura was keeping Alexander and Lily occupied.

"Are you okay?" Lily asked as soon as they got close. Worry and concern filled her face. "Laura said we needed to stay here."

"She was right. You did good waiting," Carter told her. Relief filled Lily's face. She'd been the caretaker for her younger brothers until Mia had come along. Lily was used to taking care of them, so being told to stay away would have been hard for her.

Mia brought her horse alongside Lily and patted her leg. Lily gave her a small smile.

"What happened anyway?" Alexander asked. He still looked worried for his little brother.

Carter shrugged. "She saw something and spooked."

"What did she see that scared her that bad?" Lily asked, glancing around at the meadow like something might jump out at them.

"Sweetness doesn't like snakes," Laura replied. "If she thought she saw one, she might have bolted."

"Snakes?" Mia frowned. "Isn't it a little cold for snakes?"

"It's been warmer lately, but it could have been a stick that looked like a snake," Laura replied. She frowned at the mare trailing Carter's horse. "She's usually our best-behaved horse. I would never have put him on her if I thought she'd do that."

Mia nodded. So much for Sweetness being the easy horse.

"But, Grayson did great. He kept his head and held on," Carter said. "I'm very impressed."

"I'm basically a cowboy then, huh?" Grayson asked, his grin getting bigger as he thought about it.

Carter mussed the boy's hair with his hand. "Most definitely."

The ride back was much less uneventful. Alexander tried to convince Laura to let him gallop again, Laura said no, and Alexander continued to ask. To keep him from trying to anyway, Laura had Lily and Alexander work on various riding drills and techniques.

They crested a small hill and the barn was back in sight. Mia's heart rate was almost back to normal and she no longer felt like she was running on pure adrenaline anymore.

She looked back to see Carter and Grayson whispering secrets. Grayson kept giggling at whatever Carter said. Grayson looked completely comfortable and safe with him.

Mia thought of the interview she'd read on Carter where he said he never wanted kids. It was a shame. He was so good with Grayson, Alexander, and Lily. Not just anyone could have Grayson giggling and happy after such a scary afternoon.

They were almost to the barn when Carter pulled his horse to a halt.

"Before we finish, you have to ride Sweetness home by yourself, Grayson," Carter announced.

Grayson's hands tightened and his face paled. "I do?"

Carter nodded and dismounted, leaving Grayson up on the horse by himself. He looked so small and afraid up there that Mia almost said no.

"Yes, because I don't want you to be afraid of horses." Carter reached for Grayson and picked him off his horse. He walked him over and placed him up on the gray mare's back. "I'll be right here the whole time. I'll make sure you're safe."

Grayson swallowed hard. "Okay. I trust you, Carter."

It went against Mia's instincts not to run over and rescue Grayson from this, but she was so proud of the brave face he was wearing. She also knew how important this was.

When you get thrown off a horse, you have to get back on, she thought. Even though Grayson wasn't thrown off, he was scared. This was necessary to prove to himself that he could do it.

"You ready?" Carter asked, handing Grayson the reins to his horse.

Grayson pressed his lips together as tight as they would go and gave a short, tight nod. Mia loved how brave this kid was.

Carter started them at a walk, then moved to a trot. He jogged alongside the horse, never letting go of the horse, and making sure that Grayson was in control. They made a sharp turn into the far paddock and kept running. Mia held her breath as they came around back into view.

Grayson was smiling. The fear was gone and he was enjoying the ride now. Laura moved into position just in case something happened, and Carter let go of the horse and let Grayson trot on his own.

Grayson did marvelously. He turned the horse toward Mia and his siblings and came up to them. His siblings praised him for his bravery and he beamed with pride. The fear was gone, which was exactly what Carter wanted. Carter looked rather proud of himself as they all turned to bring the horses back to the barn to groom them after the ride.

Once at the barn, the kids all rushed inside after tying up the horses to get the brushes and prove that they knew what they were doing. If they took care of the horses, they knew they would be more likely to be able to go riding again. Laura was teaching them well and Mia was grateful.

Mia brought Jasper to the fence just outside the barn and then frowned. Where the kids knew exactly what to do, it had been a long time since she'd groomed a horse. Jasper looked over at her as if to say, "what the heck lady? Get this stuff off me!"

Mia undid the saddle and fumbled with it before taking it off. It was heavier than she expected, but she got it on a nearby saddle rack with an "oof." The saddle blanket was much easier. She looked around the stall, searching for the curry comb.

"Looking for this?" Carter asked, holding up a curry comb. He walked over and greeted Jasper while he handed her the comb. "I'll help you."

"You don't have to," Mia replied, but secretly she was glad of the offer. She didn't remember exactly what to do next, so having him here would be a huge help. "Don't you have to do your horse?"

Carter worked on Jasper's hooves, picking out the dirt

and checking for stones. "The kids are taking care of Max," he said. "One of the perks of being the boss."

"Oh," she replied, picking up her brush and working alongside him.

Everything was quiet. Jasper slurped at some long strands of grass but was otherwise content to stand quietly while they groomed him. The sounds from the kids nearby were muted and soft. Mia felt hot and could tell that her cheeks were flushed as she worked next to Carter.

Having him this close was actually unnerving. She was trying her best not to think of how nicely his arms moved, or how good his jeans looked, or even just how he made her feel warm and tingly. She was becoming twitterpated and she knew it. The worst part was that she could feel her attraction to him growing with every moment they were alone together.

"Here," he offered, handing her the stiff brush. Their hands touched briefly and Mia gasped. His touch was electric and sent desire and heat straight down her spine and into her toes. She hadn't been expecting her reaction to be so strong for such a simple, accidental caress.

She looked up and straight into Carter's eyes. They were so blue and held a smolder that made her insides go gooey. It didn't help when he gave her a cocky half-grin that told her he knew exactly the effect he was having.

"You're doing great," he told her. He leaned toward her, tucking his head as though he might kiss her. Her back went against the fence post and every inch of her hoped that he would press her against the post and kiss her senseless. Yet, at the same time was nervous. It had been a while since she'd let someone other than kids into her life. Plus, she wasn't exactly feeling sexy and desirable. She was covered in horse sweat and grass, but then again, so was he.

She was past simply wanting a kiss. She wanted him to press her up against this fence post and take her completely. Even then, that might not be enough to put out the flames of desire growing in her core. If he didn't make a move, she was going to.

Instead of kissing her, he simply reached and put a grooming brush on the fence behind her before stepping back and out of her reach. Her heart was going a million miles an hour with the possibility, and it hadn't happened. Did she imagine the attraction between them? They'd come close to a kiss in the barn, but that was a week ago.

"Looks like you've got this under control," he said, his voice low and gravely. He smiled that cocky grin again that told her he knew exactly the effect he was having and was enjoying teasing her with it. "I'll see you next week."

He stepped back, leaving her wanting so, so much more. She was practically panting with wanting more. She watched, open mouthed as he sauntered away, nodded to the kids and went to speak with the security guard coming up the path toward him.

The stiff brush fell out of her hand. She'd forgotten that she'd even been holding it. Jasper nickered at her that she wasn't done grooming him yet.

Mia shook herself, trying to break the spell Carter had just put over her. She still ached to feel his touch, to taste his lips, and to release this energy. She reached down and picked up the brush, watching him walk away. She couldn't have wanted him more if she tried.

Chapter 11

arter

THE PIECE of fabric hanging from Carter's porch fluttered in the slight breeze. It would have been picturesque, if not for the words "YOUR FAULT", which were written in what could either be blood or red paint. Carter hoped it was paint.

Carter's hands shook as he came back into the house. He no longer felt safe here. He felt like running to the nearest police station and simply taking up residence. But he was done running. Whoever was doing this was going to chase him across the globe. It was best to stay here, where he could control things and make plans. He held the high ground, even if it didn't feel like it at the moment.

"Are you okay, sir?" Brian asked, coming up behind him.

"I'm fine." Carter already knew he wasn't going to be able to sleep tonight. The dreams of fire were already in his mind.

"The bomb squad says that it would never have gone off," Brian informed him. "The threading on the head of the pipe bomb wasn't tight enough."

"That's comforting." Carter turned from the open door and took a deep breath. The discovery of a pipe-bomb on his front porch with the note attached had him rattled. The fact that it wouldn't go off didn't bother him nearly as much as the fact that his enemy had gotten yet another bomb within killing range. "What other leads do you have? I want this to stop."

"We're working on it, sir. The arrest the police made last week obviously wasn't the main perpetrator. Whoever did this was smart," Brian told him. "They knew how to get past the cameras using reflective material. All that shows up on the film is a giant white spot."

The two of them stared out at the front porch as the security team buzzed around like angry bees trying to find who had broken into the hive. Carter was going to have to give a large gift to the Denver bomb squad for their assistance in removing the bomb without alerting a news team.

"And they got past the manned patrols," Carter added. His voice was hard, but inside he was scared which was exactly what the person doing this wanted. He was determined not to show how much this intrusion unsettled him. This wasn't supposed to happen here.

"I'm the head of security, but I have no idea how they got it on the porch without triggering an alert, sir," Brian said quietly. His voice was low and dangerous. He obviously didn't like not knowing. "I'm looking into it possibly being an inside job."

Carter looked out at the empty spot on his porch. That

was an unsettling idea. Who would keep him safe from his own security team? "Who found it?"

"Johnson. Ben Johnson," Brian replied. "He's one of the newer guys, but he came with a lot of recommendations. I doubt he had anything to do with this."

"Was it his patrol?"

"No, sir. This side of the house is mine. I don't trust anyone else with it." The big man's face grew hard and his shoulders somehow increased in size right in front of Carter's eyes. "This is personal now, sir. They messed with the wrong man. I won't let this stand."

"You know I trust you, Brian." Carter put his hand on Brian's shoulder. Brian was the only person Carter trusted with his security. He'd known him almost his entire adult life and the man had literally taken a bullet for him. Carter knew in his gut that Brian was going to get to the bottom of this and destroy whoever was terrorizing the ranch.

"Johnson found it as he was leaving at the end of his shift," Brian explained, stepping away from Carter. "There was a three-minute window when it could have been placed, and this is the only blind spot. Whoever did this, knows how to time the shift changes and avoid the security cameras that don't use infrared. And they knew to avoid me."

"That's concerning." Carter hated that his stomach tensed. He could almost feel the heat of the flames again.

"I agree, sir." Brian paused for a moment before continuing. "Sir, it may be time to change locations."

Carter considered it. However, the thought of leaving didn't give him hope. It made him angry. He wasn't about to be pushed around. It was time to push back.

Carter was done running.

"No. I'm staying," he said. "We catch him the next time he even *thinks* about coming on the property."

"Yes, sir." Brian pulled out a tablet and punched in a code. He held it out to Carter. "I'd like to add some new hardware to the system. More cameras, more alarms, and some of my own personal touches. Some of it will be common knowledge, but most of it will only be known to you and me. I'd usually consider it overkill, but..."

Carter glanced at the tablet and pushed the approval button for everything Brian wanted. He then looked back over at the bloodied airbag on the porch. His stomach twisted and fear gnawed at his bones.

"Do whatever you need to do, Brian. And then some."

"I will keep you safe, Mr. Williamson," Brian promised. His eyes darkened. "Whoever this is, they've just messed with the wrong man. This was my watch. It won't happen again, sir."

Carter almost felt sorry for the poor SOB who now had a very angry Brian after them. Brian's pride was on the line now.

"I know it won't, Brian." Carter handed the tablet back to Brian. "You have my full approval to do whatever you need to do."

"Excellent sir," Brian replied with a sharp nod. "I'd like to restrict the number of people who have access to the ranch. Cut it down to Laura, the two approved ranch hands, the trainer, and the vet. They've all passed background checks and have worked here long enough I don't suspect them. No one else."

"I want Mia and the kids." Carter was surprised at how vehement the words came out. Brian raised an eyebrow at him. "Unless you think little Grayson managed to carry that up here without anyone seeing him."

He motioned to the porch with the long walk up the driveway.

"Mia and the kids, too," Brian amended. He frowned at the scene. "We'll find out who is threatening you, sir."

"I want this taken care of, Brian," Carter told him. Anger flowed through his veins and he clenched his fists. "Do whatever it takes."

Chapter 12

$\mathcal{M}$ia

THE SUN slowly slid down behind the mountains, pulling them up over herself like they were a giant blanket. The sky was awash with pinks and golds that reflected off the snow capped peaks making the world look more like a painting than real life. Mia took a deep breath in and tried to save this moment. It was going to be their second to last time on the ranch, and she wanted to remember it like this.

The window was basically paid off. Even if Carter only had paid the kids the barest of wages and purchased the most expensive window possible, the work was still done. They were only on the schedule one more time. It made Mia's heart ache in a way she hadn't been expecting. She found herself looking forward to these trips. Though, if she was really being honest with herself, it was seeing Carter that she really looked forward to, not the horses and watching the kids work.

"Mia?" Laura asked, touching her arm and pulling her away from the sunset. She wore a hopeful smile. "I wanted to ask you something before I mentioned it to the kids. I didn't want to get their hopes up."

"Sure," Mia replied, turning away from the mountain view and back toward Laura and the barn. "What's up?"

"Our mare is going to give birth soon," Laura explained. "I think the kids would love to be a part of it."

"When is it supposed to happen?"

"It's hard to say." Laura shrugged. "These things are impossible to plan. The mare is showing all the signs of impending birth though, so it should be tonight or early tomorrow."

"You think they're ready for this?" Mia had already had an in-depth "where do babies come from" discussion with Lily and Alexander, and a shorter version with Grayson, so at least she knew she didn't need to go into how the baby got there.

Laura nodded. "Lily has learned everything about it already. I think she knows more about the science of it than I do at this point. She's going to make a great veterinarian someday," Laura explained proudly. "The boys have asked about it, too. I think they'd really benefit from the experience. They can all stay in the barn tonight to help."

Mia thought for a moment as Grayson and Alexander walked past the barn doors, each of them carrying horse equipment and smiling. There had been no more behavior incidents at school since the boys had started working on the ranch. Each of the kids' teachers were reporting that they were paying more attention in class and their grades were going up. Even their foster mom was reporting better behavior.

Mia smiled at her boys and then looked over at Laura. It

would be good for the kids to see something so natural, plus they didn't have school tomorrow.

"Okay. They can stay. What do you need from me?" Mia asked.

Laura grinned. "Nothing," she said. "I can't wait to tell them!"

"Thank you for inviting us," Mia replied with a smile.

"It was actually Carter's idea," Laura told her. She paused for a second. "Is there something going on between the two of you?"

Mia hoped that the heat flushing through her cheeks wasn't too obvious. "Not really, why?"

Laura shrugged. "Since the two of you have been hanging out together during the kids' work times, he's been happier. He's actually the happiest I've ever seen him."

"Really?" Warmth filled Mia's chest. "He's happier?"

"A lot," Laura told her. "And it's always when you're around. So keep coming by because I like a happy boss. I'm going to go tell the kids."

Laura grinned at her and then hurried back toward the barn, excitement in every step as she went to tell the kids that they were staying the night at the ranch to help with the horse birth.

Mia watched her. She grinned, feeling butterflies dance in her stomach. He liked her. If she were fifteen years younger, she would have gone straight home and practiced writing "Mia Williamson a hundred times in her diary.

She giggled at the idea and realized she liked the sound of her name with his. Which just made her giggle more. She was entirely crushing on him. Not only was he cute, but he made her laugh. She wondered if the kids had noticed that Mia was happier too. Because she was. She totally and completely was happier with Carter in her life.

"You're staying tonight too, right?"

Mia turned, startled to see Carter leaning against the fence behind her. She wondered exactly how long he'd been there and mentally tried to remember everything she'd just said in case she'd said something foolish. Luckily, she was fairly sure she'd only said "Mia Williamson" in her head and not out loud.

"I can't let them have all the fun, can I?" Her heart fluttered in her chest. The sunlight was in his gold hair and sparkling in his eyes. It was enough to make a girl's knees go weak.

He grinned at her and her knees really did go weak. That man had a smile that turned her to melted butter.

"What are you up to today?" Mia asked, trying to regain her composure. She was a strong, confident woman and she was determined not to go all goo-goo eyed just because he looked like sex on a stick. He pushed himself off the fence and sauntered over to the barn doors.

"Just coming to see how my mare is doing," he replied. She tried not to stare at the way his shoulders filled out his shirt. "Care to join me?"

"Sure." She hoped she didn't sound as breathless as she felt. How did he do this to her? She was a smart, professional woman, but his mere smile sent her brain spinning and her hormones into overdrive.

Side by side, they walked into the barn. He put his hand on the small of her back in the cool darkness of the barn and guided her to the birthing stall. She felt a thrill go through her at his touch and she tried not to giggle like a school girl. It was harder than she expected.

Hopeful Dreamer was inside a large stall, looking huge and ready to pop, though Mia would never tell her that. The mare's tail was neatly wrapped up and tied back out of the way and she looked at the two of them as they entered. Mia could have sworn the mare rolled her eyes at them as if to say, "Oh good, more people to watch me. Fabulous. Just what I wanted."

"I actually had some more questions for you on the car design," Carter murmured, still looking at the mare. He'd dropped his hand when they'd reached the stall and Mia found herself wishing he'd put in back on her.

"I'm happy to help," Mia replied. Her stomach got all giddy again at the thought that she had an excuse to be with him.

He motioned to a bench along the back side of the barn and together they sat down and started talking.

"What did you think of the trunk? Was the trunk size appropriate?" Carter asked, pulling up the designs on the phone.

"Depends on if you like some junk in your trunk," Mia replied automatically. She was glad the barn was dimly lit so he wouldn't see the blush cross her cheeks. She felt like the world's worst flirt, but she wasn't about to give up.

"I happen to like a little bit of junk," Carter replied slowly. "Makes driving the curves more exciting."

Mia risked a glance over at him and he winked. She giggled. She desperately racked her brain to come up with some clever car innuendo, but nothing came that made sense, so she went with actual, helpful advice.

"In actuality, the trunk can always be bigger. Especially if you're marketing to parents. I always need more space for bikes, gerbils, suitcases, and other things," Mia said, hoping she didn't sound too lame.

"Bikes, suitcases, and *gerbils*? In your *trunk*?" He sounded horrified.

It took Mia a moment, but then she remembered

hearing something sexual about gerbils and butts and she realized what she said. She *had* been looking for an innuendo, so she just decided to go with it.

"Some of my kids have gerbils," she informed him. "Why? Were you thinking about gerbils in my trunk?" She fluttered her eyelashes innocently at him. "It's quite an experience."

Carter made a choking sound and quickly cleared his throat before looking over at her.

She gave him an innocent smile. "We're just talking about cars, right?"

"Right." He shook his head and put the phone back in his pocket. He'd clearly given up on the innuendo game, and she was glad. This was not her flirting forte. He smiled at her and leaned back against the wooden barn wall. "Do you know why I'm building this car?"

"I'm guessing it's for the chicks," Mia replied. "Chicks love cars. Cars with trunks."

"Definitely for the trunks." Carter chuckled. "And carrying gerbils."

"So, why are you building this model?" Mia asked, trying to get back to a conversation that didn't make her want to wash her brain out with soap. "You said this one would be an electric like your other models, but far less expensive. Plus, this design doesn't scream 'luxury car' like the other models do."

"I want everyone to have a safe, reliable, and awesome car," Carter explained. He paused for a moment before continuing. "I've been toying with this idea for a long time, but a little over a year ago I finally saw how important this was."

"What do you mean?" Mia asked. She liked how close he was sitting on the bench with her. It was doing strange things to her insides that had her wanting to scoot closer to him.

"A young woman died in one of my vehicles. It was an older model and they'd tried to upgrade it with my new airbag system, but something went wrong. The accident killed her. If she'd been driving a safer car, that woman would still be alive." Carter's eyes focused on the far wall, but that wasn't where he was looking. He was looking into his past and seeing the dead.

"I'm sorry to hear that," Mia said softly. She put her hand on his and gave him a squeeze. He didn't pull away, so she kept her hand there.

He took a deep breath that seemed to shake the distance from him. "Accidents happen in cars," Carter said. "I want to offer my technology to everyone in this car so these accidents don't happen. Especially just because someone can't afford a better car."

"That's very noble," Mia told him.

He looked over and smiled at her. "Noble? You're the one literally saving children. That's noble."

Mia blushed. "I'm just doing my best to help."

"If these kids are any indication, you're doing a good job." Carter smiled. "Other than the whole window thing."

"Yeah," Mia agreed. "But, you'll notice we haven't had a single window incident since, so we're improving."

Carter laughed. He still hadn't pulled his hand away or made any indication that he was going to do so. She wondered for a moment what it would feel like to have him touch other parts of her and her body warmed.

"Is this what you always wanted to do with your life?" he asked her.

For some reason she wasn't sure of, Mia paused before giving her usual easy answer of "yes, of course!" She looked at his blue eyes and felt something inside her want to give the real answer.

"No," she said slowly. "I mean, helping kids is what I've always wanted to do with my life. Especially disadvantaged kids and kids in the system with no one else. I want to help them, but the being a social worker isn't my dream job."

Carter raised his eyebrow. "So what do you want to do?"

Mia bit her lip. She didn't usually tell people this, but she felt a connection with Carter. He told her about his desire to build a safer more affordable car, she could at least tell him her reasons for wanting to do more than just be a social worker.

"I want to help more kids. I want to do so much more than what I can legally do now," Mia explained. "As a social worker, I'm trained not to get too close. I have paperwork and bureaucratic issues that I have to do. I want to do so much more, but my hands are often tied. I have to do what the system says, not what's necessarily needed."

"What's the dream then?" Carter asked.

"I want to open a camp for foster kids," she explained. "A place for kids to come for a season and have an experience that builds them up. I want to fill in their educational gaps, find solutions to behaviors, and give them a positive experience with resources they can use for the rest of their lives. I want to give kids a chance. I want them to taste success, so they know it's possible."

"What's stopping you?" Carter asked.

"Funds. Time. Support." Mia shrugged. "Most of the kids I want to help aren't the cute little kids that look good on a poster. They're usually the kids with bad pasts and records to match. It also takes a lot of money, and right now, the system is always short. Something like what I have in mind would take millions of dollars and never be profitable. I don't have enough experience with charities even to get started. I don't even know *where* to get started."

Her hand was still on his. She could feel the heat from his body and now that she was talking about something she was passionate about, she was suddenly very aware of how warm she was. And how warm he was.

"Anyway, it's a pipe dream," she said with a shrug. "So, right now, I'm just doing everything I can to help the kids I can reach."

"Can I help?"

She turned sharply to look at him. His blue eyes were wide and open and he had a small smile at her surprise.

"Um, sure," she sputtered. She knew he wasn't going to be a future foster parent and as a business owner he didn't have a lot of spare time to donate, but as a billionaire, he did have money. "A lot of the kids in foster care don't have anything to call their own. We always need back-to-school supplies, toys, suitcases and stuff like that."

"I'll see what I can do," he replied. "You can count on me."

"Thank you," she said with a smile.

He pulled out his phone and quickly typed something. Her phone vibrated a second later, indicating that she'd gotten an email.

"I sent you my charitable donations person," he said, putting his phone away. "You tell her what you need, and she'll see that you get it. I want to help. I'll donate as much as I can."

Mia stared at him for a good ten seconds with her mouth hanging open. She knew the offer wasn't just a casual one that would be taken away. The internet article on him said that he was big on donating huge amounts of money. She just hadn't ever expected to be a recipient.

"I tell Laura to keep the barn clean, but you're going to catch flies like that," he teased, reaching up and putting his thumb and forefinger on her chin. He pushed up gently, helping her close her mouth.

It was prime kiss position. Everything in her gut said to go for it. He wasn't pulling away, and in fact seemed to be tipping his head and bringing her chin to him. Her whole body heated with desire. She closed her eyes just as their lips were about to meet.

"Mia! We got pizza!" Grayson shouted.

Mia's eyes shot open and she pulled back. Carter looked as startled as she felt. He sat quickly back and Mia knew that they had just missed their kiss by seconds. Again.

"Are you two coming? We can't eat in the barn," Grayson said, coming up to the two of them and grabbing their hands. He was completely oblivious to what was going on.

Carter chuckled and shook his head before standing and following Grayson. He held the barn door open for her.

"One of these days, there won't be an interruption to save you," he remarked as she walked past him through the door.

"Who says I want to be saved?" She looked back just in time to see Carter's pupils dilate and his mouth go into the cocky half grin that she loved. With a grin of her own, she hurried to the house to eat her dinner.

Chapter 13

arter

EVERYTHING WAS quiet in the black of the night. The barn was dark and the only sound was the gentle breaths of breathing creatures. Moonlight softly filtered through an open window and the electric lantern was turned down as low as possible while they waited. Carter was sure that he was the only one awake in the entire world, and right now, that was okay with him.

Mia was sleeping on his shoulder. He didn't dare move, despite the fact that his nose itched, his right foot was asleep, and there was a piece of straw poking at his left ankle. The last thing in the entire world that he wanted was to wake her up and have her move away from him. The way her body pressed against his, even just platonically, was heaven.

He smiled at her as she slept. They'd been sitting on the bench, talking about the kids and cars and various other topics. The conversation had drifted back to his cars, and she'd asked him some questions that took a while to explain. He'd started talking and realized she hadn't said anything for awhile. He'd looked over to see that she'd closed her eyes and drifted off to sleep on him. He hadn't dared to move since.

One of the kids murmured something in their sleep. Carter stretched his neck out as far as he could to see if they were still okay. He couldn't see anything and no other sounds came from the dark. All three of the kids were asleep in the hay of an empty stall. They'd fallen asleep hours ago since nothing was happening yet.

Mia shifted slightly and Carter held his breath. She settled further on his shoulder with a small, contented sigh. It made his stomach do funny things and his heart speed up. She was the last person he would have picked for himself to fall for. She wasn't in his social circle, she didn't know anything about cars or horses, and she didn't want him for his money. Yet, she made him happy.

He was falling for her and falling hard. He reached over and brushed a strand of rich brown hair from her face. She was beautiful in a fairy-like way. She would never grace the cover of a magazine or strut down a runway, but she was stunning nonetheless.

Not to mention she was funny and smart. He smiled more in the time since he'd met her than he thought he'd smiled his whole life. His cheeks hurt after their days together from simply smiling. She made him happier than he'd felt in years, and she did it without even realizing she was doing it.

He loved that the connection between them was so mental and not just physical. Although, dear lord, did he want her physically too. Those "almost" kisses were devastating. They were all he could think about. The cold showers were getting out of hand, but it was all he could do to stop himself.

He took a deep, steadying breath. The last thing he needed to be thinking about with her touching him was her kisses. Or what her skin felt like. Or how her eyes darkened when she looked at him. He was already imagining her in his bed and how her hair would splay across his pillow...

"Did I fall asleep?" Mia mumbled, sitting up and shaking her head slowly. "I'm sorry."

Now that she was sitting up, she wasn't touching him anymore. He hated it.

"Don't worry about it," he replied. He reached down and moved the poking piece of straw and scratched his nose. "It's past midnight and we've all had a busy day."

"Anything with the mare yet?" she asked, looking around at the dark stall.

He shook his head. "Nothing yet."

She stood up and stretched. He tried not to stare at the sliver of skin on her belly that showed when she raised her arms and curved her back. It brought back the thoughts of what her hair would look like on his pillow and he didn't want to take a cold shower right now. He stood up, trying to shake some feeling back into his legs.

"The kids are totally out," she whispered, peeking over at them. "Alexander is snoring and Grayson is curled up against Lily."

"They passed out about an hour ago," he replied, focusing his gaze on the children and away from her. How was it that moonlight somehow made her more beautiful? Now, he was thinking of the moonlight on her hair on his pillow. He shook his leg, forcing himself to focus on the pins and needles sensation instead of thinking about her naked body glowing in the moonlight. It was a struggle.

"Is there anything to drink?" Mia asked, glancing around the barn. "I'm parched."

"Other than the watering troughs?" Carter joked. She stuck out her tongue at him and he laughed. "There's a pot of coffee at the house. I'll come with you."

She grinned at him and stretched once more, making his thoughts go back to moonlight and bare skin. It took all his willpower not to just push her up against the barn wall and kiss those perfect, smiling, red lips of hers. By the time he focused, she was already halfway out the door.

He grabbed the walkie-talkie and followed after her. He managed to only check out her ass a little as they walked in the moonlight. He was only human after all.

Chapter 14

*M*ia

THE STARS and crescent moon shone brightly against the dark sky as Mia walked through the dark to the house. Fall was definitely on its way. The night air was cold and crisp and she found herself wishing she'd worn her sweatshirt from the barn. The thin material of her shirt was not enough outside tonight. It wouldn't be long before the frost and snow arrived from the high country. She shivered.

And then, suddenly she was warm. Carter placed his flannel jacket over her shoulders. It was still warm with the heat of his body. She looked up at him surprised, but he just smiled at her and kept walking to the house.

She followed behind, pulling the collar around her. The jacket smelled like him. It smelled so good that she caught herself burying her nose in the fabric and taking a deep sniff in while he wasn't looking. She decided he was never getting his coat back now. It was warm and it smelled good. It was hers now.

Carter held the kitchen door to the main house open for her. Welcoming yellow light poured out into the darkness, beckoning her inside. The kitchen was not a traditional farm kitchen. It was a big, gourmet kitchen that belonged in a magazine, not a farm. Everything was made of clean lines and granite, with enough counter space to make three Thanksgiving meals and not run out of room.

Mia kept the jacket on, even though the room was comfortable and warm. She leaned against the counter by the sink as Carter picked up the stainless steel coffee pot and frowned. He shook it gently before peering inside.

"I'll make a fresh pot," he said, setting the empty pot down. "Laura must have beat us here. Will you hand me the coffee? It's on the shelf behind you."

Mia turned and opened the big glass cabinet door and grabbed a bag of coffee. Being in the kitchen with Carter felt so domestic and comfortable that she didn't even have to think as she handed the bag to him. Their hands touched.

She didn't let go of the bag, but neither did he. Their eyes met and she unconsciously licked her lips. He stepped toward her, coming into her space. Her breath was coming fast now, but it was full of excitement. They were toe to toe, with the hand with the coffee coming to rest on the counter beside her. His free hand went to her neck and his hips pressed into hers. The bag of coffee fell to the floor.

This time, there were no interruptions. There were no children to stop them at the last moment, no horses, no nothing. Just the two of them and that kiss.

His lips found hers and she melted into him. His hips pressed her into the counter and she wrapped her arms around his broad shoulders. He was strong and solid under her touch. His kiss enveloped her and heated her core more than coffee ever could. She moaned softly into him.

The sound of her desire inflamed him. He put his hands on her hips and lifted her up onto the counter so he could kiss her better. Her legs wrapped around his waist and he fit there like a puzzle piece with the counter supporting her ass. She shrugged the jacket from her shoulders, wishing they could just be naked *now*. Clothes were stupid. He kissed down her throat, nibbling at her like she was the most delicious thing he'd ever tasted.

His tongue and teeth on her delicate skin made her gasp and tighten her legs around him. She tried to think of a way that both of them could get their pants off without having to let go of him. His touch was driving her crazy.

She reached for the hem of his shirt and pulled it up over his head. His muscles flexed in the kitchen light and she lost her ability to breathe. He was gorgeous. The comfortable shirts he wore hid muscles that belonged to a Greek god. She ran her fingers across his skin and tried to touch as much of him as possible.

It felt so good, she could barely believe this was happening. It had to be a dream. There was no way that she was making out with Carter in his kitchen with his shirt off.

He reached up under her long-sleeve t-shirt, his fingers going slowly up her stomach and pausing at the satin of her bra. A low, deep, and primal noise came out of his throat that made the space between her legs heat.

"Carter? Where are you?" The walkie-talkie crackled.

"Ignore it," she whispered, tucking her chin to his shoulder and kissing the skin there. Good lord, he tasted amazing. His kiss, his skin, it all tasted like heaven and she wanted all of him.

"Carter, it's happening," Laura's voice crackled over the walkie-talkie. "The hooves are out. Where are you?"

They both paused, skin touching.

Mia knew how much he wanted to be there for the birth of this foal. She swallowed hard and pulled back slightly. He was panting, his hair mussed from her fingers and eyes dilated. He hadn't pulled away from her yet, but he wasn't moving anymore either.

"Where are you? Come quick!"

Mia released her legs. He kissed her once more before steeping back. He moved like he might change his mind and miss the birth just to take her on the kitchen counter. She helped make the decision easier by jumping off the counter and handing him his shirt from the floor.

"That was definitely better than coffee," she said, watching as his muscles flexed and moved as he put the shirt back over his head.

He grinned at her as soon as his head cleared the shirt. His hair was still messy and his lips looked swollen and in need of more kisses. She was seriously considering going for another kiss when the walkie-talkie chirped again.

"Laura says you have to hurry!" Lily's voice crackled into the room. Laura must have handed it off to her to assist with the birth.

"Next time," Carter promised, handing her his coat from the counter. The way he said it made her blood pump and her core heat. There was a hot promise for a lot more than just kissing with clothes on and Mia wanted it. She wanted it bad.

"Hurry!" Lily's voice came over the radio again.

"I'm going to hold you to that," Mia said as they both hurried out of the kitchen and into the dark of the night.

Chapter 15

M *ia*

MIA STOOD IN THE STALL, taking it all in and enjoying the quiet that came after the birth. Lily was still asking both Laura and the vet questions about the birth process and the science of what had just happened. She was so excited it looked like she might never sleep again. The two boys had passed back out in the hay again.

Carter was in the birthing stall watching the foal. The little stallion stood on wobbly but determined feet. He was working on getting his walking legs steady. Carter stood off to the side, watching him with proud eyes.

He'd make such a good father, the thought came to Mia. She shook it away. He didn't want kids.

She turned from him and checked on the boys. They had woken up and been excited to watch the birth. Alexander said it was gross and Grayson's eyes had gotten bigger than Mia had ever seen, but they'd done well. They'd certainly learned something and she was glad they'd experienced the miracle of life. It was something she'd never seen before either.

She found some blankets and put them over her sleeping kids. Grayson never stirred, but Alexander murmured something about, "horse babies" with a smile on his face. Mia chuckled and shook her head. It certainly was an experience they would never forget.

She brushed some hay from their hair and stood up. The vet was explaining something about using artificial lights to push back the fertile period of mares and how that could change gestation time. They were able to have foals in the off season using this method. Mia's hand went to her own stomach without thinking. The aching loss filled her soul.

What would it feel like to carry a child?

She would never know. There would never be a child in her belly.

She thought she was over the hurt the thought left in her. She thought she had come to terms with the fact that she would never grow a child within her, but for some reason, it hurt tonight. Maybe it was that she'd just watched the mare become a mother, or perhaps it was the sweetness of the kids, but today, the loss hurt.

Mia turned and faced the barn wall, forcing herself to take deep even breaths. She blinked back the tears that stung at her eyes and tried to remember that she was okay with this. She wasn't meant to have children and she'd accepted that. It had taken time since finding out, but she'd come to terms with her body.

The overall memory of finding out had faded, but there were still details that stood out. The coldness of the room, the crackle of the paper on the examination table, the poster describing different kinds of birth control on the wall.

She'd had an unplanned pregnancy in college, but miscarried. It was the miscarriage that the doctors were concerned about. They'd run tests. She'd been asked to come in and speak to a doctor directly. She remembered how warm the doctor's hands were as she comforted Mia with the news. Mia had always thought it strange, considering that medical professional's hands were always cold.

She could never get pregnant. There was something wrong with her anatomy. The fact that she'd even gotten pregnant once was amazing. It would never happen again.

The news had ended the relationship. He'd wanted kids. She wanted them too, but he wasn't willing to adopt. In hindsight, it wouldn't have been a good match, but at the time, she'd felt like everything had fallen apart. Her world was destroyed.

It was part of why she was so adamant in her work. She would never have children of her own, but she was going to do her best to help everyone else's children instead.

Three more deep breaths and she felt in control again.

Alexander mumbled something again, shifting in his sleep under the blanket. Mia leaned over and picked another piece of hay from his dark hair and smiled. These are her kids. She didn't need to have them within her to love them.

She made sure they were tucked in and comfortable before heading back to the birthing stall. Lily was still learning everything she could from the vet and luckily the vet looked interested in teaching. They'd moved on to the anatomy changes required to facilitate a birth. Mia shook her head and looked for Carter.

He was sitting in the hay with the little sleeping foal in

his lap. Carter beamed up at her as she approached, his eyes glowing with pride. He was as proud of this little horse as if he had fathered it himself. Mia smiled at him. He should be proud. His favorite mare had given birth and he'd been there to help.

"Come here," he whispered as the little foal's eyes flickered with dreams in his lap.

Mia knelt in the hay and reached out to touch the small creature. He was so perfect. He made her heart ache again, but in a different way this time. He was beautiful and loved, which was all she ever wanted for any child.

Hopeful Dreamer nickered softly as if to say, *Isn't he wonderful?*

Mia reached out and stroked his soft coat. She couldn't agree more. He was wonderful.

Chapter 16

*M*ia

MIA WAS POUTING and she knew it. She didn't like that she was pouting, but she wasn't about to stop. She was committed to the pout now and there was nothing that was going to change it. It was the last day on the ranch. The sun shone as if nothing was changing. The breeze blew colder, but still, it didn't feel as if everything were coming to an end. The kids were grumpy and worked slowly as if taking more time to do their chores would make their time here last longer. They were pouting, too.

Mia wasn't going to miss having to rearrange her work schedule to fit in these trips, but she was going to miss just about everything else. She'd found herself looking forward to these visits, not for the time on the ranch, but because of Carter. He'd made these days brighter and the best parts of her week.

She wasn't sure how she was going to see him again. The kiss in the kitchen still burned in her thoughts, but it was just a kiss. After the birth of the horse, they didn't have a chance to discuss what had gone on. Now, it was a day later and she wasn't sure what to do about it now.

She wanted to see him again, but with the kids no longer working on the ranch, she didn't exactly have a good excuse to come out here and see him. So, today, she'd dressed up in the sweater that she knew made her look good, her best jeans, and took the extra time to fix her makeup before coming. If today was their last day, she was at least going to feel confident and look good. Even with a pout.

Carter was busy with work when they'd arrived, so Mia had gone to her favorite spot just outside the barn to watch the kids while she waited. She closed her eyes and tried to focus on how good the sun felt on her face. It was hard to pout when the sun felt so warm.

"You going to miss us?" Carter asked, coming up behind her. She smiled, and turned her face from the sunshine to look at him.

He wore a dark blue shirt that brought out the color of his eyes. His hair was mussed by the wind and he wore that cocky smile that she loved. She vividly remembered the way he tasted, sweet and delicious, and the way his body felt pressed up against her. It took all her willpower not to just drag him off behind the barn to finish what they'd started the other night.

"Maybe," she teased, doing her best to give him a nonchalant shrug. He raised his eyebrows and she couldn't help but laugh. "Okay, definitely. I didn't think I'd enjoy spending my afternoons watching my kids haul horse feces around, but, I'll miss the company."

She met his eyes and loved the way he lit up at her words.

"I was actually hoping to talk to you about that," he said with a smile.

"About horse feces?"

Carter laughed. "Kind of. With the new foal, we can use a few more hands around here. Would your kids be interested in a job? Laura already has Lily half-trained to her position and has been asking me if we can keep them on."

"You're offering my hooligans a job?" Mia asked.

"I'm hoping their social worker might think it's a beneficial program for them," Carter replied. "That it will enhance their social skills and provide physical activities unavailable elsewhere."

Mia's heart lightened. This wasn't their last day on the ranch. She looked over at the barn to see Alexander pause and sigh wistfully before continuing with his duties. He looked so sad that she wanted to run over and tell him the good news right then. Instead, she grinned at Carter.

"I think I might be able to make something work," she said, her smiling giving away her excitement. "*I* might need some extra convincing, though."

"Could I possibly convince you over dinner?" Carter asked.

Her heart fluttered and the nervous energy of a romantic encounter flooded through her. "Dinner?"

Carter nodded, his eyes fixed completely on her. "You, me... someplace that isn't a barn. Food that isn't a pizza."

Mia's stomach was already doing excited flip-flops. "I'd like that."

Carter's grin deepened. When he looked at her like that, the idea of going back to the kitchen for another kiss was the only thing she could think of.

"Good," he said, turning to walk off back toward his garage. "I'll pick you up Friday at five."

Mia stared at his back for a moment before her brain kicked in. "What should I wear? Where are we going?"

Carter glanced back over his shoulder and grinned, but didn't stop walking. "You'll see."

"You'll see?" Mia repeated quietly as she watched his very nice backside go around the corner. "What the heck kind of answer is that?" she called out, but he was already gone and not giving her any answers.

It was Friday at four and Mia had no clue what to wear for this date.

Her small bedroom looked like a tornado hit it. Clothes were scattered and flung in all directions, with at least four different outfits currently on her bed. Fancy, casual, sporty, fun? There were a million "not pizza" places that would require vastly different outfits. Mia groaned and tried not to think about what she was going to do with shoes.

She wondered if FEMA helped with disasters like this.

The doorbell rang. Mia shot daggers at the front door and sighed with frustration. It was too early to be Carter, but she wasn't in the mood to deal with solicitors or neighbors. She huffed and stomped to the front door to find it was the package delivery guy.

"Sign here," he said, holding out an electronic signature device. She scribbled something that vaguely resembled her signature and took the box. She wasn't expecting anything, especially not something that she had to sign for.

After thanking the delivery man, she went back inside and closed the door to her apartment. As soon as it latched, she ripped open the box. She pulled out a layer of tissue paper and tossed it to the side with a gasp. Inside was a gown made of purple sparkles. She pulled it out and batted off the tissue paper nestling it the box. It was floor length and absolutely stunning.

But that wasn't all that was in the box. Tucked beneath the tissue paper was a set of matching purple heels. She pulled them out and read the designer label on them. Jimmy Choo. She nearly dropped them, and then felt bad. The shoes were worth more than two months of rent. She was almost afraid of what the dress was worth.

She searched for a note to explain the dress and the shoes, but there wasn't one. There was only one person she knew that had the money to send her something like this. Carter's words floated into her mind.

"You'll see," he had said. Well, she definitely knew what she was wearing now.

"Oh, Carter," she whispered, shaking her head. This was above and beyond what she had even thought possible. She played with the fabric, running her fingers over the beautiful iridescent purple dress. "Where in the world are you taking me?"

She grinned and went to her bedroom to put on the dress. It fit like it was made for her and she tried not to think about how he had gotten her size so perfectly. She went to the full-length mirror hanging on her closet door and gasped.

The dress was magic. It made her look like something out of a fashion magazine. It hugged exactly the curves that needed to be hugged and hid the curves that didn't. She didn't know her boobs could look that amazing. She stared at the mirror.

"I really could be on a billionaire's arm," she whispered.

She wouldn't even feel out of place or like she didn't belong there. For the first time, she could actually see herself being with him, and not just at the ranch. She could be a billionaire's girlfriend.

She did a little turn and checked her watch. She had just enough time to do her makeup and put her hair up into something that better matched the dress's formality. She paused at the mirror one more time before heading to the bathroom, and a flicker of uncertainty went through her.

"Where the heck are you taking me?" she asked the mirror. A dress this nice deserved something amazing. She grinned. Wherever it was, she was going to look fabulous.

THE DOORBELL CHIMED. This time, it made Mia grin and race to the door to get it. She opened the door, fully expecting to see Carter. She had a feeling he'd be wearing some sort of fancy suit and look like a million bucks. She was rather excited to see how he cleaned up.

But, he wasn't at the door. She tried not to show her disappointment to the uniformed man standing at her door.

"Ms. Amesworth?" the man asked. He wore a crisp blue uniform with matching hat. "Your transportation, ma'am."

He turned and motioned to a huge stretch limo taking up half the apartment complex's parking. Mia's eyebrows went up in surprise.

"Just let me grab my purse," she told him, reaching inside and picking up her small handbag. It was the nicest one she owned. It was a knock-off, but it looked real enough that she hoped it wouldn't look too strange with the dress.

She followed the uniformed driver out to the limo. As she walked, she could hear blinds going up as people peeked out of their windows to take a look at who the limo was for. The neighbors were going to be talking about this for weeks. Her cheeks heated slightly, but she carried herself proudly. She'd learned a long time ago it was better to fake it than look nervous. Especially in heels.

The driver held her door open, and she did her best to get inside gracefully. She opted for sitting first and swinging her legs into the car after her since that seemed to be the easiest way not to rip the dress or flash the neighbors.

Inside, blue neon lights filled the spacious interior. The seats were leather, and there was a single rose in a small vase. She sat primly, with her hands and purse in her lap as the driver started the car and maneuvered out of the apartment complex.

"Where are we going?" she asked the driver as he pulled out onto the highway leading out of town.

"I've been instructed not to tell you, ma'am," the driver replied with a small tip of his head. "It's not far, though."

"Okay." She smiled at him and just tried to take everything in. The last time she'd been in a limo was for a fundraiser several years ago. Although then, she'd had to share it with six other people, so it hadn't been quite this comfortable. She looked around, trying to take in all the details so she could tell her kids and answer their questions about what it was like to be in a limo. She knew they would want to know what color the seats were, if the windows rolled down, and what all the buttons did.

The driver was right; the drive wasn't long at all, and soon he pulled into what Mia assumed was an empty field. She frowned as she looked out and didn't recognize anything.

"We're here, ma'am," the driver told her, opening her

door. She slid forward to the edge of her seat, and there was a hand waiting to help her out.

She took it and stood up, only to find that the hand belonged to Carter. She nearly fell on her face he looked so handsome. She was used to seeing him in jeans and t-shirts with his hair windblown and face scruffy. Today, he was wearing a soft, dark blue suit and his hair was brushed neatly in place. He'd shaved, so there wasn't even a hint of a five-o'clock shadow on his perfect face.

"You ready?" he asked, smiling as he helped her steady herself. High heels on the dirt of the field didn't help with her balance.

"Sure," she replied with a grin. She looked around and didn't see a building for them to go in. "What are we doing?"

Carter chuckled and nodded to something behind the limo. She turned around to see a small plane waiting in the empty field. She nearly fell down again.

"Something amazing," he promised, helping her navigate the field toward the runway. "And don't worry, I already cleared it with your boss."

"My boss?" Mia asked, confused. "What does my boss have to do with this?"

Carter grinned, his eyes sparkling mischievously. "Didn't I tell you this was an overnight adventure?"

"No, no you didn't," she replied. She gave him a gentle push on his shoulder. "And how did you find out my boss's number?"

His grin got wider. "I'm a billionaire. I can find anything out."

She laughed at his pride and then focused on navigating the field in her heels. He helped her up into the stairs into the airplane. Mia felt like a celebrity walking up the steps to the door where a stewardess in a fashionable dark blue uniform greeted her.

The inside of the private jet was not what she expected. Instead of rows of utilitarian seats, there was a white leather couch, two reclining chairs with a table, and from what she could see, a full bar in the back. It wasn't a plane as much as it was a flying apartment.

"This is unbelievable," Mia said, looking around.

"I wanted to take the helicopter, but it just doesn't have the fuel range. This is faster." Carter squeezed her shoulders as he passed her to sit on the couch. The flight attendant handed him a flute of champagne before he even had time to get comfortable.

"Fuel range? How far are we going?" Mia asked. She had no idea how far a helicopter could go, but she figured it was a long way. Just how far were they going?

Carter just smiled at her, keeping his secrets.

"Champagne?" the attendant asked, offering Mia a glass.

"Um, sure." Mia accepted the glass and sat next to Carter. Close, but not so close that the flight attendant would get any ideas.

"Cheers," Carter said, holding up his glass. Mia tapped hers gently against his and took a sip of the bubbly liquid. This all felt so surreal, she was sure that she was imagining things. She heard the engines start to purr and the plane moved onto the runway.

"You don't have to worry about the kids or work tomorrow," Carter told her over his champagne. "I made sure they were all taken care of. I want you to have fun."

"I'm in a private jet," Mia replied with an excited giggle. "I'm already having fun! Thank you, Carter."

She reached out and touched his hand. He grinned and held her hands in his. She giggled and laughed, feeling as if she were already flying. She was grateful for his hand, since she was still a little nervous. This was her first time on a private jet, after all.

"You ain't seen nothing yet," he promised. And with that, the plane took into the sky.

Chapter 17

arter

THE VEGAS SKYLINE came into view with all its lights and brilliance. For a moment, Carter wondered if he'd overdone things, especially for a first date. Taking a girl to Las Vegas was a bold move, but he'd wanted to do something that Mia would never forget. He wanted to do something amazing for her, and this was the first thing that had come to mind.

He looked over, afraid she'd be overwhelmed only to find her with her nose pressed to the window like a little kid. She looked over at him and pointed to the city, her eyes full of excitement. She bounced up and down in her chair as she peered back out.

Nope, he decided. Definitely didn't overdo it.

He loved seeing her like this. She was so excited and happy that it filled the cabin with infectious enjoyment. This was the happiest he'd felt in months. He wasn't thinking about cars or horses or his business with her beside him. He was thinking about her and her happiness. It was something he could certainly get used to.

The dress certainly helped him keep his thoughts on her. He still couldn't get over how amazing she looked in it. When he'd seen the color, he'd known it was the dress for her, but he had no idea just how stunning she'd look in it. The word "stunning" didn't do her justice. She was elegant and sexy, bold and beautiful. He was having a hard time not staring.

The plane came in for a smooth landing, and there was barely even a bump as they touched down. She was grinning from ear to ear, her face lit up with the neon lights of the city as they exited the steps down off the plane.

"Vegas?" She spun around on the tarmac, giggling with excitement. "We're in Vegas!"

"Have you ever been before?" he asked as he guided her toward their waiting limo.

She nodded. "Once. It was for my friend's twenty-first birthday. We got the cheapest flight out, stayed in this super sketchy hotel and lost all our rent money on blackjack."

He grinned. This trip was going to blow that out of the water. He'd picked well.

"Why are you smiling?" she asked, sliding into the limo with grace.

His grin just got wider. "I have so much to show you," he replied.

Chapter 18

ℳia

MIA WAITED until Carter wasn't looking to pinch herself. She did it three times in different places just to make sure that she wasn't dreaming. This trip to Las Vegas was more than she ever could have imagined.

First, there was dinner at the Gordon Ramsay Steakhouse. Except, Carter had them in a private room with the chef preparing and delivering all six courses personally. When she joked that it should have been Chef Ramsay feeding them since it was his restaurant, he actually called the Chef up and had him talk to her.

Then, he'd gotten them front row tickets to the newest Cirque du Soleil show, complete with backstage access to meet the performers and see how the incredible stage worked. She didn't even know that such a thing was possible.

Now, they were walking into the Bellagio hotel, and she was ready for anything. At this point, she was half-expecting to have her name spelled out by the iconic fountains out front. There didn't seem to be anything that Carter couldn't do.

The lobby to the casino was extravagant and beautiful. Mia hadn't been to the Bellagio before, so she stared in awe at the beautiful artwork and marble floors. Carter let her stare. He walked slowly beside her, obviously enjoying her reaction to seeing the hotel for the first time.

A bride in a big, beautiful wedding dress walked past with her groom on her arm. Mia and Carter stopped to let them pass by. The bride was grinning from ear to ear as they walked past and Mia couldn't help but grin right back at her.

Mia motioned with her head to the bride. "Is that what's next on the itinerary?" she teased.

Carter shrugged. "Do you want it to be?" He grinned that cocky, self-assured grin.

She was expecting him to vehemently deny it, so when he didn't, she wasn't quite sure how to respond. Most men she knew would have balked and run away from the marriage offer.

"All it takes is a phone call," he said, pulling out his phone and waving it in front of her.

Mia knew he was just teasing. Or at least she hoped he was teasing. They were nowhere near the point where they should be discussing marriage. This was their first date, for crying out loud, yet her heart was still pounding. Half of her was hoping he'd say yes. That half of her wanted to fling caution to the wind and marry this man because she was falling in love with him. She liked him more than she had liked anyone in a very, very long time.

"So, am I calling Elvis or what?" Carter asked. He put on his most cheesy salesman-esque smile that made her laugh.

"I'm going to say no," Mia replied. She wondered if that was a flicker of disappointment she saw on his face or just her imagination. "But only because you haven't properly asked."

Carter chuckled and put his phone away. "I'll keep that in mind. Next time, I'll ask properly."

Mia's heart skipped a beat. He said there would be a next time. The idea made her insanely happy, and she wasn't quite ready for it. A blush heated her cheeks and made sure to take his hand as they walked through the lobby.

Carter walked right past the front desk and kept going until they were in a fabulous lounge. Hand stitched leather walls with a warm walnut wood trim made the room look gorgeous and inviting. The view of the beautiful gardens outside only added to the room's charm.

"Mr. Williamson, it's a pleasure to see you again," a woman greeted him, coming out from behind a desk. This had to be a private lounge for the high rollers, Mia assumed. The woman smiled at them. "Your room is ready if you are. If not, fresh champagne is available here in the lounge."

"We'll head on up, thank you," Carter replied.

"Right this way, sir," the woman replied with a warm smile.

She led them to a private elevator and pressed the button. It was quite possibly the nicest elevator Mia had ever seen. It zoomed up the fifty floors fast enough to make her ears pop. When the doors opened, the hostess led them out to a large door. She opened it and held the door open.

"We have everything set to your specifications, sir," she said as Mia and Carter walked in. "If you need anything, please don't hesitate to ask. Again, my name is Kari. Thank you for choosing the Bellagio."

Carter thanked her, and she left them to explore the hotel room on their own. Mia had a feeling that Carter had been here before. He certainly seemed to know his way around the place.

The room wasn't just a hotel room. To call it that was a disservice. It was more home than hotel. It was certainly bigger than her apartment and far more luxurious. Everything was beautiful and soft, rich and inviting. She felt like she could live here comfortably for the rest of her life and never want for a thing.

"May I pour you a drink?" Carter asked, going to the main table. Champagne and strawberries were set out, along with an impressive display of fresh flowers. She nodded.

"This is amazing..." Mia looked around the room, still amazed at the richness. This room must have cost a literal fortune. "Sometimes I forget that you own a car company."

Carter chuckled and popped the cork on the champagne like a pro. He then expertly poured them each some champagne into crystal champagne flutes.

"There are some perks to owning your own business," he replied. He held up the glass of champagne, and she carefully clinked hers against his. "To us," he toasted.

"To us," she repeated with a smile. The champagne tickled her nose as she took a deep sip. She assumed it was expensive, but all champagne tasted alike to her.

Mia walked to the huge window overlooking the strip. The lights of the city, as well as the dancing fountains, filled her vision and she stared in wonder. The strip lit up the darkness and twinkled in the night. Anything was possible in Las Vegas, and this view proved it.

"Do you like it?" Carter asked, coming up beside her.

"I love it," she replied honestly. She turned to look at him, his face handsome in the light. "Thank you."

She looked up at him and felt her body heat. They'd been so busy enjoying Vegas that this was the first time since the limo they were actually alone. She licked her lips, remembering the kiss back in the kitchen. Her body ached to have that kiss again, to have him touch her like that again.

His face split into a slow smile, but she kissed him before the smile could complete itself. He tasted like champagne and everything she'd ever wanted.

He set his champagne down and dove into the kiss, his hands going to her hair and pulling her into him. His tongue quested inside of her mouth, seemingly searching for more of her. Mia moaned, so quietly that it could barely be heard. That just seemed to spur Carter on more, and he leaned into her, bending her back.

"I've wanted this all day," he said. "I want you."

The words made Mia's entire body seem to tingle. "I want you, too," she replied.

He smiled, then pulled back a little bit. "I do have one last surprise for you this evening," he said.

He turned and put his hand back in his pocket as if he was going to make a phone call. Mia grabbed his tie and pulled him back in for another kiss, and he pulled his hand out of his pocket. "It'll have to wait," she whispered into his ear.

"Yes, ma'am," he said with a smile. She put her hand on his chest and kissed again, feeling his heart rate increase as she became more assertive. This time, she leaned toward him, and as she moved her hands to his sides, she made sure to catch his suit coat and move it off his shoulders, letting it fall to the floor.

Carter's hands moved to the bottom of his shirt, where he began to undo his buttons, all while still kissing Mia. When he got to the top of his shirt, he began to loosen his tie. Again, Mia grabbed his tie and stopped him. "Keep it on," she said, surprised at her own tone.

He grinned from ear to ear and popped his collar, slipping the tie from the shirt to his skin. Then he took a step back, throwing the shirt off in a dramatic motion. For a moment, Mia marveled at the hard body in front of her. This was clearly a guy who not only rode horses but also spent a ton of time at the gym.

"Wow." Her mouth watered at the sight of him.

He smiled. Then stepped forward and his hand touched the fabric of her dress, sending shivers through her. "You know, when I saw this dress, all I could think about was how good you'd look in it." Mia smiled and blushed a little bit. He continued talking. "But now, I'm afraid the only thing I can think about is how good you'll look out of it."

Mia couldn't help but giggle a little bit. She reached back to unclasp the back, but in a moment his hands were around her, reaching up her back. "Please, allow me," he said as if he were the perfect gentleman for offering to disrobe her. She felt him deftly release the clasp, as sure of himself as when he uncorked the champagne. He moved the zipper down slowly, agonizingly slowly.

As soon as the zipper was at the bottom of her back, he leaned down and moved his lips to her neck, kissing down to her shoulder. She could feel his stubble against her skin, and it felt incredible. His hands moved to her shoulders, gently moving the straps of the dress.

With a whisper, the dress fell to the floor, leaving her in nothing but her panties. For a moment, she thought about covering herself, but she stopped herself. She knew this was coming and had never felt so comfortable in front of a man. She wanted to be seen by him.

Carter took a moment to feast his eyes on Mia's body, before returning to her neck and kissing downward. He trailed his kisses across her shoulder to her collarbone, working his way down to her breast. As soon as his tongue met her nipple, a shiver of pleasure ran down her body. She moved her hands to the back of his neck and pulled him in tighter, loving the feelings coursing through her.

Carter seemed overcome by lust as he moved his mouth back up to Mia's to kiss her. In one smooth motion, he leaned down and grabbed her butt, lifting her up and into his arms as he began to walk. Mia squealed a little bit as she wrapped her arms around the back of his neck. His hands were kneading her butt cheeks, obviously enjoying the feeling of it.

Mia didn't know where they were going until he leaned down, gently falling on top of her in the bed. Without hesitation, he began moving down. He grabbed her breasts, pushing them up a little bit and looking up at her. "These are amazing," he said.

"Thanks," she said, unsure of what else to say. No one had ever called her breasts amazing, but she definitely appreciated the compliment. He began sucking on one, and then the other, enjoying her body. She began to writhe with pleasure. It was incredible to feel this wanted, this desired.

He moved down even further. She had picked a conservative pair of panties, sure that the panty lines wouldn't show underneath the sparkly purple fabric. He didn't seem to mind as his kisses began to trace the edges of her underwear. There he stayed, going back and forth, making sure to avoid the fabric directly over the space between her legs.

She whimpered, unable to control her arousal. She

began to move her body, trying to get him to apply pleasure to her throbbing clit. Just a little would be enough to keep her sane, she thought. He dodged her attempts, though.

"You can't just shove it in my face. You have to ask," he said, then went back to kissing.

"Do it," she moaned. She didn't need to tell him what she wanted. She knew he understood.

"And you have to ask nicely," he added, looking up at her and smirking.

She felt like hitting him, but then he lightly moved his chin so that it just barely touched the fabric directly over her clit. "Please. I want it. I want it so bad." The words spilled out of her, out of her control.

He smiled, then moved his mouth to the fabric covering her opening. She almost screamed as he applied a gentle pressure. Even just this was enough to send her over the edge. She gripped the bed sheets and felt her legs squeeze shut, Carter didn't stop, though. He kept applying pressure, back and forth on her clit, as she continued to come.

When it was over, her legs relaxed on their own. She felt him taking the opportunity to put his fingers inside the fabric of her panties, pulling down. She lifted her butt to help him, not wanting him to slow down for even a minute. However, when they were finally off, there was a pause. She opened her eyes to find out what was up and saw him admiring her body once more.

There was only one way to sum up his look. Hunger.

When he saw her looking at him, he dove back between her legs. This time, there was no buildup of anticipation. His tongue was on her clit, licking as if she were the last oasis in the desert. She threw her head back and closed her eyes again, gripping the bed sheets for dear life as he sent wave after wave of pleasure through her.

His tongue was magic. She didn't know that pleasure like this was possible, but with every lick, with every nudge of his tongue, he showed her more. Just when she thought she'd reached the height of ecstasy, he would touch her and send her to another level of bliss.

"Carter," she whimpered, as she felt him start to kiss down, down her legs, pausing to kiss her feet which gave one last orgasmic twitch. Her eyes opened back up just in time to see his pants fall to the ground. He quickly pulled down his boxer-briefs, and she saw what he was working with.

"Wow," she thought to herself. He immediately began to stroke it as he looked at her, obviously enjoying what he saw as much as she was enjoying what she saw. As he stroked it, she saw how hard he was. She was still in a post-orgasmic glow, but she knew that this was going to be worth the wait.

He bit his lip. "This is embarrassing."

She laughed. "I don't think you have anything to be embarrassed about."

He laughed. "No, you goof. I'm not embarrassed about this." He gestured down and made a few thrusting motions. Mia couldn't help but chuckle at him. "You don't happen to have a condom in your purse, do you?"

She bit her lip. She hadn't even thought about it. "No, but..." she looked up at him. "You didn't bring one?"

"I did. I left them on the plane," he admitted. He looked at the nightstand and grinned.

"What are you doing?" she asked, as he picked up the phone.

"Calling Kari," he said, not finding what he was looking for at first. "The woman who escorted us up here."

Mia got a wry smile on her face. "I'm pretty sure she won't let you screw her without a condom."

Carter looked at her like he thought she was serious for a moment, then rolled his eyes at her. "Har har. No, what I meant was, she'll get us a box of condoms. It's one of the perks of staying here. They get you things." He peered down at the phone, looking for the right button to push.

Mia bit her lip. "She doesn't need to bother."

"What do you mean?" he asked, looking back at her.

"I mean, I don't want to wait. I want you. Now." She spread her legs a little further as if to show what she wanted. She definitely saw him twitch at the sight.

He gave her a crooked smile. "Yeah? You're on the pill?"

Her smile faded for a moment at the question. It would only be a little white lie, but there was no need to ruin the mood with her medical history. She couldn't have children, and she trusted him. They didn't need a condom.

"Basically," she said, only feeling a little bit guilty.

He put the phone back in the cradle and grinned at her.

Their conversation apparently hadn't dampened the mood at all, and he was still hard as a rock as he crawled back on the bed. He moved his head between her legs, giving her one, last, wet lick across her opening. She gasped, then giggled with anticipation.

He finally came face-to-face with her, kissing her deeply. She loved the way his skin felt against hers. His hands wrapped around her back as he positioned himself at her entrance. He was poised to enter her, but he paused.

Mia began to squirm. "Please," she whispered. She bucked her hips, trying to press against that delightful hardness. "Please," she said again.

Carter smiled again. "I can't say no to a lady when she's begging like that," he said. He leaned forward, and they moaned together as he slowly entered her. "Oh my God," he whispered, pulling out and pushing back into her, this time all the way in. Mia couldn't help but cry out in pleasure as he filled her completely.

"More," she whispered.

She felt his muscular arms move from behind her back. He placed one on either side of Mia's body and looked into her eyes as he began to thrust faster. Mia had never felt this kind of lust, this kind of intensity while making love before, and it was too much for her to bear. Her body tightened around him, pulling him deeper inside of her.

"Oh God Mia, if you do that then I'm going to come quick," he said through gritted teeth. The thought nearly made her come undone. She wanted him, but she wasn't ready for this to end.

"I have got to see you on top of me," he said.

Mia smiled and nodded. With one swift motion, he thrust deep inside of her and rolled his body, moving her on top. She squeaked a little and then giggled again. He began to thrust slowly, then put his hands on her breasts and pushed her up to a kneeling position. When he pulled his hands away, she moved her own hands to her breasts, cupping them as she began to writhe.

His hands went to her waist, and with those strong arms, he began guiding her up and down. She looked down to see him drinking in the sight of her body.

Suddenly, he reached up and grabbed her by the small of her back, pulling her down to press against him. His hands went to her ass, grasping her and spreading her open as if he were trying to drive even deeper into her body. As full as she felt, she didn't feel like he had much further he could go.

"I want you," she whispered, losing herself in the moment. "Come inside me," she said, surprised at her own words.

Carter didn't seem to need much encouragement. His hand went to her hips, rocking her back and forth while thrusting upward. She felt his pace increase as he used her body for his own pleasure. She wanted it.

"Mia," he gasped as he lost control. His eyes dilated, and he lost himself to her pleasure, filling her with himself. She could feel her own body reacting.

He started withdrawing from her body, and she put her hand on his chest. "No. Stay for a moment," she said. His face softened into a gentle smile as she leaned forward and rested her head on his shoulder.

They snuggled like this for what seemed like an hour but was probably closer to five minutes. She felt Carter soften and eventually slide out naturally, and she whimpered as he did. She knew she'd have him again like this, though. Hopefully again and again.

Carter moved his lips to her ear. "Do you mind if I show you that surprise now?"

She laughed. "Does it mean I have to move?"

"You might have a better view if you at least come to the window."

Mia put on a fake pout and got up. She could already feel the mess inside of her and knew she'd have to take a shower soon.

Carter got up and went to the closet, pulling out two robes. "You'll find that these are the second softest robes in the world," he said. "Plus, they come heated."

She laughed. "Wow, I'm impressed. What are the first softest?"

He pointed at another casino. "Mandalay Bay. Damned if I don't stay there at least once a year just to steal a new robe."

Mia laughed at the absurdity of a billionaire needing to steal a robe. "What's this surprise?"

"Oh yeah." He went to his phone and picked it up, dialing a number and just saying, "Now."

Suddenly, it sounded like a cannon was going on outside. The Bellagio fountains went off, spraying water higher than she had even seen them. He came up behind her and wrapped his hands around her. "That's how hard I came."

She turned around and slapped him in the chest. "Stop it!"

He chuckled, pulling her into him, so her back pressed against his chest. Together, they watched as the water danced and spun to music and light. It was magical.

"Should I be looking for anything special?" she asked, hoping she wasn't missing something important.

He laughed. "I don't think it can spell someone's name or anything. It's just a special show, just for you." He dipped his mouth to kiss the curve of her neck into her shoulder. "But if it could, I would do it for you."

A happy warmth filled her, and she leaned back into him. He kept his arms wrapped tightly around her as they watched their personal water show. This definitely had been a night to remember.

Chapter 19

 arter

CARTER STRETCHED out in the darkness and felt warmth beside him. He looked over to see Mia still sleeping peacefully beside him. Her hair was spread out across the pillow just like he'd imagined so many times. Heat twisted in his belly, a desire to feel her touch yet again, but he didn't want to wake her. She looked so beautiful and peaceful that he almost didn't dare to breathe for fear he might disturb her.

For the first time in his life, he had everything he ever wanted.

His phone chirped with a message, and he quickly scrambled to silence it. He read it his blood ran cold.

 Urgent security issue. Need to speak to you immediately.
      -Brian Cards

CARTER GLANCED ONCE MORE at the sleeping beauty next to him and sighed before getting out of bed. Brian wouldn't message him unless it was very important. He sighed once more, rolled out of bed, and slipped into one of the pre-heated robes from the closet.

He texted Brian to come into their suite as he closed the door to the bedroom behind him and went to the kitchen. A full breakfast was already laid out, complete with french toast, pancakes, waffles, fruit, eggs, and other breakfast delights all on heated trays and ready whenever they wanted. Carter went for the coffee first.

He had just sat down at the table with his cup of caffeine when Brian walked in. The big man's face was dark and dangerous.

"What happened?" Carter asked, taking a sip of coffee.

"The ranch garage was set on fire," Brian said, sitting across from him. Carter nearly spit out his coffee.

"What?!" Not only did Carter have some of his favorite cars in there, but he also had several of his projects including the newest car he showed to Mia. It was all backed up on cloud storage, but the loss of the garage would be a blow to his creativity.

The fact that it was fire made his stomach turn to stone.

"The fire system caught it before it did any damage," Brian quickly added seeing Carter's panic. "But there was a message burned into the side of the wall."

Brian set his tablet on the table and pushed it toward Carter. A picture of the garage was on the screen. The words "YOUR FAULT" were burned into the side of the building, along with some blackened edges and scorched wood along the beams.

Carter was glad he was sitting down. His blood wasn't pumping right, and he was having difficulty staying calm. If he had been home and not on this trip, he would have been in that garage. It was where he spent all his time, and he often slept in there when he wasn't working with the horses. He would have seen the flames again.

He carefully took another sip of coffee, using the motion to buy him some time to think. His mind was lost to the flames for a moment before calming himself. It wasn't the same as before. Still, the fear gripped him. He'd never been so happy to be in Vegas.

"Are there any leads?" he asked after a moment.

"We have a possibility, sir." Brian reached for the tablet and swiped to another screen. "It's been a lot of leg work. The messages seem to indicate they blame you, and we've been exhausting all legal issues related to the cars. We've got a couple of possible suspects, and the police are working closely with us. We're cross-referencing it with everything we had from the office bombing. With any luck, we'll have answers soon."

"Thank you, Brian," he said. There wasn't much evidence to the office bombing to compare anything to, unfortunately. Every part of the bomb was available at a regular gas station, and they had no video footage. The cameras were blocked, so nothing usable was recorded. Carter sighed and took another sip of coffee. At this rate, he was going to need another cup soon. "Is everything still good for today? I want to show Mia the high roller experience."

"Yes, sir," Brian said with a nod. "The hotel security has been a pleasure to work with, yet again. I hope we managed to stay unobtrusive last night?"

Carter nodded. "I don't think she even realized you were here. Good job."

"My pleasure, sir." Brian stood from the table. "Is there anything else you need, sir?"

"No, thank you."

With a curt nod, Brian turned and left the room. Carter stared into his empty coffee cup and tried not to think about his garage. He tried not to think of the flames. It wasn't so much the things that were in it, but rather the fact that it was where he thought himself the safest. He hated the feeling of vulnerability.

"Everything okay?" Mia asked, opening the door from the bedroom and peering out. "I thought I heard your security guy."

Her hair was still messy with sleep, but she'd found the heated robes and had wrapped it around her small frame. She looked so beautiful, Carter had a hard time not staring.

"You did hear him," Carter replied. He stood up and came over to kiss her cheek. She smiled at his touch, and it made his heart less heavy.

"What's he doing in Vegas?" Mia asked, heading toward the coffee pot with enthusiasm. Carter followed behind her to get his second cup.

"Watching out for us," Carter explained. "We've had security the whole trip."

Mia finished pouring her cup and looked thoughtful before nodding. "That explains the bathroom."

"The bathroom?"

"When I went to the bathroom at the restaurant last night, I could have sworn I saw Brian duck into the kitchen. At the time, I thought I just needed to slow down on the wine, but it must have actually been him," she replied. She took a sip of her coffee and sighed with pleasure. She took another before continuing. "Why do you need so much security? I mean, I know you're a billionaire, but it seems like a lot."

Carter carefully finished pouring his cup before answering.

"Do you remember when I told you I was hiding out on the ranch? The reason is that there have been some serious threats on my life." He tried to keep his voice light, like it wasn't a big deal. Still, he hated the way her face paled, and her eyes grew big with concern.

"Oh my god," she whispered, setting down her cup. "Why would anyone want to hurt you?"

He liked that she thought him innocent and undeserving of threats.

"People blame me when something happens with their cars," he explained. "I get quite a few death threats."

She nodded slowly. "I understand the security then," she said. She frowned and picked up her cup again. "Why would they blame you? You didn't cause the accident."

Carter shrugged. "I'm an easy face for them to blame. And they need someone to be responsible for their pain," he replied. "Most of the time, it's not even the fault of my cars. I can't keep passengers safe when they don't wear seat belts or run into telephone poles."

"Most of the time?" She took a small sip of coffee, her dark eyes watching him. He sighed.

"Remember that case I told you about? The one where the woman died due to a faulty airbag?" He played with the cup in his hand, staring into the dark liquid. "Her family is pressing more charges, filing more lawsuits. I would too, in their situation."

"That's not your fault," she assured him. "You said they put an airbag in her car that was faulty. You didn't do that."

"It was my brand of car and my brand of airbag. It was supposed to be safe," he said, turning away.

Carter heard the clink of her mug sitting on the granite bar. She moved to be directly in front of him, placing her hand on his cheek. He leaned into her touch.

"Carter, that's not your fault." Her dark eyes were serious. For a moment, he almost believed he was completely blameless.

"Let's talk about something else," he said, kissing her fingertips. "It's a beautiful morning, and I don't want to talk business today. We're vacationing."

Mia grinned and snuggled into his chest as he wrapped his arms around her. He tipped his head and kissed the top of her hair, smelling her sweet shampoo. How did she manage always to smell so good? It had to be some sort of magic. He kissed her head again, and she hummed with pleasure.

"You like that?" he said, his voice getting a husky quality. That noise had his thoughts going south.

"Mmm hmm," she murmured, pressing against him. She fit into him like she was his missing piece.

"I think I know another way to make you hum," he told her. She looked up at him with a naughty twinkle in her eye.

"I like you so much, I'll even wait on breakfast for that," she said. "And breakfast smells good."

He chuckled. "You must like me a lot."

Mia grinned and stepped away from him. She winked once and then sauntered toward the bedroom. He didn't know how she managed to make a fluffy robe look sexy as hell, but somehow she did. Her hips had a magic power over him when she moved like that.

With a grin of his own, he set down his coffee cup and ran after her. Breakfast could wait.

Chapter 20

M *ia*

FORTY-EIGHT HOURS IN HEAVEN. That's what the weekend was to Mia. It was bliss. She'd never had a weekend so relaxing, revitalizing, or amazing. She hated that it was over because she never wanted it to end. She never wanted this alone time with Carter to end.

The plane started to descend as they came in for a landing. Mia had never noticed before, but the empty field behind the ranch house was actually a runway. Not having to go to the airport was definitely a perk to dating a billionaire. Mia held Carter's hand, wishing they could just stay up in the air forever. It wasn't Vegas that she was going to miss, it was having him all to herself.

He'd showed her Vegas as only a billionaire could. They'd eaten the most amazing food she'd ever had in her life from beef Wellington to sushi to gourmet chocolates. They'd gambled at the high roller tables with celebrities.

Carter told her most of it was comped, but she didn't even want to know what their spend had been.

The best part was the time they spent up in their suite. Much of it was in the bedroom, but it wasn't all just sex. They'd talked and laughed until she was crying with joy. They'd both put their phones away and just spent time with one another.

Mia hadn't even missed her phone. Carter was amazing. He had this unique ability to take something serious and turn it into something hilarious. He was witty and kind, and he always put her first. It made for the best weekend of her life.

Now, she felt like Cinderella returning home after the ball. Except she still had her prince. That made her smile as the plane landed with a soft thump. She wasn't missing a shoe, and her prince charming knew where she lived. She was better off than Cinderella.

Carter held her hand as they exited the plane. Going down the stairs, even with no one around, still felt luxurious and elite. She felt like she should wave to the paparazzi, even though all there was around them was grass and a couple of pine trees. The air was cold, and there was a tang to it that told her snow was on the way. It was now fall in the mountains and winter was coming.

Once down the stairs, she turned her phone back on and together they walked back toward the ranch house. Her phone immediately buzzed with a message.

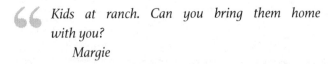

> *Kids at ranch. Can you bring them home with you?*
> *Margie*

MIA FROWNED as she read the message from the kids' foster mom. Today wasn't one of the kids usual work days, so she didn't know why they were here. The fact that Margie had dropped them off but couldn't pick them up was also strange.

"The kids are here," Mia told Carter, putting her phone away. "Did you know they were here?"

"No," Carter said shaking his head. "Laura must have needed some extra help. I should check my phone. I turned it off."

"I know." Mia grinned at him. "I appreciated it too. It made this morning much more fun."

He grabbed her hip to spin him to her and kissed her full on the mouth. It was only a taste of what happened this morning, but it heated Mia up better than a fire. If the kids weren't at the ranch, she would have gone for another round.

"Next time," Carter promised. Apparently, he was thinking the same thing. She loved the naughty grin he gave as he released her and they walked to the barn.

"Alexander, did you find the extra curry combs?" Lily asked as they walked in.

"Yes, I put them in the stalls like you asked," Alexander replied as he hurried past with his arms full of supplies. He smiled as Carter and Mia walked in, hurrying over to give them both a hug hello.

"Where's Laura?" Mia asked, looking around the barn. The manager was nowhere to be seen, which was odd. She was always so good about being where the kids could find her.

Lily walked over slowly. She had a clipboard and a serious look on her face.

"She called me this morning totally freaking out," Lily explained after greeting them. "There's been an accident."

Carter stiffened, and Mia could see him pale. He reached for his phone and quickly began fumbling with the buttons.

"Is she okay?" Mia asked, concerned. From the look on Lily's face, Mia had a bad feeling she wasn't.

"Physically, she's fine," Lily replied. She sighed and fiddled with the clipboard. "Her parents were in an airplane crash early this morning."

Mia's heart sunk. There was no way that the next words out of Lily's mouth were anything good. Lily looked up at her and Carter with tears in her big brown eyes.

"They didn't make it." Lily swallowed hard and looked at the floor. "I was here helping her when she got the news."

Mia hugged Lily to her. The girl leaned into her, sniffling but keeping strong.

"I have to go help with arrangements," Carter said. His voice was hollow. He patted Lily on the back, obviously still in shock himself. "Thank you for being here for her."

He gave her shoulder a squeeze and looked at Mia.

"Go," Mia whispered. She now felt guilty about having him keep his phone off all morning. He cared for Laura, and she knew that he was worried about her. He was a good boss.

"Thank you, Lily." Carter nodded and patted Lily's shoulder one last time before pulling out his phone and heading into the house to see what he could do to help.

"Are you okay, Lily?" Mia asked, keeping her arms around the girl until Lily let go of her. Lily nodded and wiped her eyes.

"I just feel so bad for Laura. She's got a younger brother and sister." Lily looked over to where her brothers were busy cleaning one of the stalls. "I can't imagine having to tell them."

Mia's heart broke. Lily and Laura had grown close these past few weeks, and Mia knew how much Lily respected and looked up to the other woman. She pulled Lily back into her for another hug. Lily didn't resist, which told Mia that the teenager needed the affection. Mia wrapped her arms around her tighter and rubbed her back. It didn't take away the pain, but it was soothing.

"Is Laura going to be okay?" Lily asked her voice a whisper into Mia's shoulder.

"Laura is strong," Mia assured her. "It's going to be rough, but she'll get through it. You're doing a good thing helping her here."

Lily smiled up at her and took a deep breath. She pulled away, and Mia knew that she was going to be okay, too.

"I'm glad I can help," Lily told her. "I'm glad Alexander and Grayson can help, too. Between the three of us and the trainer, we'll keep things running for her. She taught me most of what she does, so I can at least keep things under control. It's one less thing she has to worry about for the moment."

Mia warmed with pride. "You are all such good kids."

Lily rolled her eyes but smiled and blushed. She shrugged and resettled herself. "Did you have fun on your weekend away? Margie said Carter took you someplace."

Lily grinned. "He took me to Las Vegas. It was amazing."

"Vegas? Nice," Lily said. Her eyes narrowed. "So, are you two a thing now? Please tell me you married him there."

Mia laughed. "I did not marry him." Though, she

thought of his offer and felt butterflies. "But, you want to know if we're dating?"

"Yeah." Lily nodded. "Are you?"

"I think so," Mia told her, thinking back to the weekend. They'd never officially discussed it, but there was no way after the weekend they'd just shared that they weren't some sort of couple.

Lily grinned. "Good. He's good for you, Mia."

Mia looked at her surprised at her bluntness. "Thanks."

"I'm going to get back to work," Lily informed her, pointing to her clipboard. "Do you think we can stop and pick up some food to bring to Laura's house on the way home?"

"Definitely," Mia promised.

"Thanks," Lily said with a grin and then turned and started helping her brothers with the barn chores.

Mia was impressed. Lily was growing up so fast and doing a great job at it. She looked calm and collected as she checked her list and made sure that the barn and the horses were taken care of the way Laura would want. Mia had a feeling Laura would be pleased with the results. She made a mental note that Lily would need to spend more time here, as would the boys.

The idea of spending more time on the ranch made her happy. She wished it had come about differently, but she was going to take advantage of the opportunity. More time at the ranch meant more time with Carter. She looked over at Lily working one last time before pulling out her phone and looking for restaurants with takeout on their way to Laura's house.

Chapter 21

*M*ia

MIA SAT at her desk and rolled her shoulders, trying to get the knot in the back of her neck to relax. There was still so much paperwork that needed to be done, as well as a special project from her boss she'd just been told about today. It felt like she still had hours to go, but it would never be enough.

Today had been a rough day. She'd been to court with one of her other kiddos, and it hadn't gone well. Her heart hurt with how much she wanted to help, but couldn't do to lack of resources. The kids needed and deserved so much more than she could give.

She sighed and tried not to look at her phone. She wanted to reach out and talk to someone but wasn't sure who. Carter had messaged her earlier in the day, but he was busy, and she didn't want to bother him. All of her friends were working and wouldn't be able to talk. She sighed and decided just to try to finish her work.

Mia checked her watch. Her boss needed her to stay late tonight to work on a special project. She didn't know what it was, but her boss didn't make the request often, so she was doing it. Even though it was a Friday night. If she could just get through some of the paperwork before it was project time, she'd feel better about the week.

Her phone buzzed, and Mia hoped it was Carter. She quickly reached for the phone to see it was just a message from her boss.

 That project I told you about- he's here.

MIA SIGHED and tried not to feel discouraged, but the last thing she wanted was to work with another kid tonight. Not after her day in court. She needed a win today, and she just didn't have the energy to fail again. She wished there were more resources and options for the kids she looked after. If she could, she would adopt every single one of them so they could succeed.

So, if there was a kid that needed her help tonight, she was going to do it. She might sigh now, but this was her life's work, and even though she felt burned out today, she wasn't about to let another kid down. He'd be here in a minute, so she focused on getting one last bit of paperwork done.

"Hi, Mia," Carter greeted her.

Mia's head whipped up from the desk, and she grinned. This was a much-needed surprise, although poor timing. Her project would be here any second.

"Carter," Mia greeted him warmly. She stood up from

the desk and kissed him. All she wanted to do was curl up in his arms, but that wasn't in the cards today. "I'm afraid I don't have much time. My boss is sending over a project for me. But, it's so good to see you."

Carter nodded and looked around. "So, this is where you work?"

"Yeah." Mia followed his gaze, noting the drab gray cubicles and flickering florescent overhead lights. It wasn't exactly glamorous. "This is where I do my paperwork. I try not to have the kids in here too much."

Carter's eyes went to the stack of paperwork on her desk. "Wow. That's a lot of paper."

"Yeah, and this is with our new 'paperless' system. You should have seen it last year." She sat down in her chair with a sigh. "I'm sure I've killed an entire forest."

Carter watched her for a moment, and she wondered just how exhausted she looked. "What's wrong?" he asked.

"I wish I could do more." Mia pointed to a stack of folders on her desk. "Every one of these kids needs something, and I wish I could do it all. I hate having to say that we don't have the funding or the personnel or the time. It kills me. It's the part of the job that I hate."

"I'm sorry," Carter said simply.

She sighed and ran a hand through her tangled hair. Her project would be here soon, and she needed to get some energy. She did her best to smile. "I'm sorry. I'm just frustrated. Today isn't going the way I planned."

Carter walked around behind the desk and put his hands on her shoulders. His strong hands instantly found the knot between her shoulders, and he started massaging it out. She groaned softly at his touch, letting herself relax for just a moment. With him here, she could feel her energy slowly coming back.

"Maybe I can help," Carter offered.

She smiled but shook her head. "I told you, I have a project coming."

"I'm the project," he told her, stopping his hands for long enough to bend to the side to look at her shocked reaction. She stared at him, and he chuckled at her expression.

"How are you a social work project?"

"Well, not me exactly," he amended. He grinned. "I set it up, so I'm the one who is going to tell you about it."

She looked at him, waiting for him to explain what he meant. This was not what she was expecting at all. "When did you set this up? How did you set this up?"

"Your boss and I talked about more than just giving you a day off to go on a trip with me," he said, shrugging and looking far too proud of himself. He held out his hand to help her up. "Come with me."

She had no idea what he could possibly have planned, but it was definitely better than paperwork. She took his hand and stood, not letting go once she was up. She didn't want to let go of him.

He took her around the row of cubicles to the entrance of the staff bathrooms. Mia frowned as they came to a stop outside the doors. The office was mostly empty, so she had no idea what they were doing here.

"Go in," Carter told her, nodding at the bathroom.

She gave him a strange look but did as he asked. She paused at the door, looking back at him and his knowing smile before opening the door.

The bathroom was completely transformed. A hairstylist and makeup artist had taken up residence at the sink counter, and there was a beautiful new gown hanging from the stall door. She'd never seen so many lights in a bathroom before.

Carter's head popped through the door, watching her expression.

"Have fun," he said. "I'll see you in twenty minutes for what comes next."

And he closed the door and left her to get pampered.

Chapter 22

arter

CARTER SAT in an uncomfortable office chair, playing on his phone for the twenty minutes while he waited for Mia in the bathroom. He spun around in lazy circles, wearing out the poor bearings in the chair and doing his best to distract himself with emails and phone games, but his mind kept going back to Mia.

She was something special. He'd never met anyone like her, and even what he had planned for her today wasn't enough. He wanted to help her fulfill her dream. He wasn't quite sure how to go about it, but if anyone could figure out how to make something work, it was Carter Williamson.

He looked up as the bathroom door squeaked, and Mia stepped out. It was worth the wait. It always was with her.

His eyes went up and down her body not just once, not twice, but three full times. He didn't even feel guilty about staring. She was absolutely stunning. The gold dress fit her perfectly and made her look like a movie star. Her brown hair was curled up and pulled into a complicated looking knot at the back of her head. He wanted to take her home and keep her for himself, but he'd worked too hard on this to do such a thing.

"This is amazing, but why am I dressed up?" Mia asked. She grinned at him, and he lost his breath for a moment. That smile lit up a room.

"You are going to a fundraiser," he explained, standing up. His stomach was twisting with excitement to see her reaction to what he had set up. He'd been working on it for the past week and had pulled out all the stops.

"A fundraiser?" she asked, smoothing the gold satin of her dress. "A fundraiser for what?"

He handed her the invitation for the event. It was printed on golden paper that matched her dress with an elegant script that screamed high-society and money.

"All proceeds go to foster kids," he said as she looked it over. "Your kids are the benefit."

Her mouth fell open, and her hand shook slightly. "How did... but..."

He loved that she was speechless. She seemed always to have something smart to say, so the fact that she had no words was exactly what he was looking for. He took advantage of the moment by giving her a quick kiss.

"It's at the theater downtown, so you'll need to head over there to schmooze and wow the guests," he told her. Given how beautiful she looked, that wouldn't be hard. "I have everything set up, so all you have to do is smile and thank them for their very generous donations."

She frowned, her brown eyes looking over him. "But you're not dressed. Are you not coming?"

He shook his head. "Security. I can't go." He wished with

all his heart that he could. He wanted to be the one on her arm tonight. He wanted to walk around with her and make her smile and then take her out of that dress. But, his security team said it wasn't possible.

"I'm by myself?" She sounded nervous, and her hand reached up to play with her necklace.

"My business partner will be there," he explained. "Ethan White is your date this evening."

Mia bit her lip. "You set me up with someone else?"

Carter stepped forward and touched her hair with his fingers. She was so damn beautiful it hurt. "He's under strict orders not to fall in love with you."

"Poor guy," she said, looking up at him. "I'll try not to break his heart. I can't help it that men fall for me whenever I smile."

"I certainly did," Carter told her with a grin of his own. He loved the color that filled her cheeks, and he tried not to think of the implications of what he just said. He was certainly falling in love with her, but he wasn't ready to declare it, and certainly not at her office just outside the employee bathroom. To cover himself, he quickly pulled out his phone and called up a picture of Ethan. "This is him. He'll meet you there."

She studied the picture for a moment and then smiled. "You sure you can't come with me?"

He was so tempted. So incredibly tempted. He'd wear the jeans and polo shirt he had on right now and borrow a tie there, but his security team would be furious. There had been another threat, and he was risking a lot just coming to her office. Vegas was built for the wealthy, so keeping him safe there had been easy. An affair like this was just too easy to breach.

"Go have fun and get some donations for your kids," he said, putting on a happy face.

She looked him over and then kissed him. It was soft and gentle. He didn't want to mess up her makeup, but she felt so amazing that he didn't want to stop either.

"Thank you, Carter," she whispered once they'd broken their kiss. "I don't know what else I can say to tell you how grateful I am."

He smiled and kissed her cheek. "Then just go have fun."

She grinned. "Thank you. Thank you, so, so, so, so, so much."

"Get going," he said, putting his hands on her shoulders and gently pushing her toward the door. If she stayed much longer, he was going to do something he'd regret.

He watched her walk down the hallway and to the exit door.

"A limo!" she shouted as she saw what was waiting for her outside. He chuckled, enjoying her excitement. She really had no idea how much money he had. A limo was nothing, but it made her day. It was adorable and incredibly endearing to see her reactions to things he thought of as normal.

She made his heart light. She made him smile just by thinking of her. He went to the glass doors and watched as the limo pulled away. He could see her inside, grinning and excited as she talked to the driver. He wished he was in there with her with every molecule of his being.

Chapter 23

M*ia*

MIA STOOD in front of the Paramount Theater in Downtown Denver and tried to take deep, steady breaths. Even the outside of the building was decorated and beautiful. There was even a red carpet rolled out along the big white 1920's style theater. She could hardly wait to see what the inside would look like. There was a sea of limos and fancy cars surrounding the place, and Mia could only imagine the amount of money coming to an event like this.

"You must be Mia," a male voice greeted her. A tall man in a tuxedo walked over with a smile on his face. He looked just like the photo Carter had shown her with dirty blond hair in a casual style and bright green eyes.

"You must be Ethan," she replied, holding out her hand. He shook it firmly before offering his arm to escort her inside. She took it but found herself missing Carter. Ethan was great, but she wasn't in love with him.

"So, we're at the half million mark, and..." he informed her as they walked the red carpet. She froze, and he nearly pulled her over. He quickly turned to face her. "What's wrong? We'll get up higher, the evening's just beginning."

"No, no..." Mia shook her head. He thought she was concerned that it wasn't enough money when just the opposite was true. "You said we're already at half a million? Already?"

He nodded, and she thought she might faint right there on the red carpet. That was so much more than she'd ever thought possible. She felt ready to cry tears of joy.

Ethan chuckled and realized she was happy. He took her arm again. "And that's just the start."

Ushers opened the big heavy doors to the theater and Ethan took her inside. Everywhere she looked were people wearing beautiful, fancy clothes and servers walking around with champagne and ornate appetizers. Carter must have spent a fortune on this, and it was all for her.

"Carter made sure everything is taken care of," Ethan explained as they walked in. "He's expecting a minimum of two million raised tonight."

Mia froze again, but this time Ethan was a little more prepared and didn't keep walking. He smiled at her shock and waited for her to find words again.

"What do I need to do?" she asked after a moment. She was ready to sell her soul for that much. That much money would help so many kids. That much money would go so far towards making their lives better.

"You don't have to do anything," Ethan told her. "Just smile and tell these nice folks how much their donations are appreciated. Carter's taken care of everything else."

Mia needed to kiss Carter. The thank you she said earlier was in no way close to telling him how grateful she was for this. She needed to kiss him and tell him a million times how much this meant. He had no idea how much she needed this today.

"We'll go over and talk to the Vanderbilts. They are a large donor tonight," he said, taking her arm and guiding her further into the party. They took a couple of steps, and it appeared the Vanderbilts were busy, so he stood off to the side. "We'll find the Tudors instead."

"Thank you, Ethan," Mia said, giving him a smile. "I don't know any of these people."

"That's why Carter sent me. I do these fundraiser things all the time, though usually in Colorado," he replied. He smiled and cleared his throat. "I hear that you have become a regular on the ranch."

"Yes. Three of my foster kids help out with the horses," Mia said with a nod. "They've really stepped up since Laura had to take some time off."

"Laura?" Ethan' voice cracked slightly on her name. His whole body froze as if her name had power over him.

"Do you know her?" Mia asked.

"I met her once."

Mia raised her eyebrows. There was so much more to that statement than he was saying. His body language was screaming that he had a crush on Laura and there was much more than just a simple meeting. She was about to ask him about it, but the Vanderbilts spotted them.

"Ethan," Mrs. Vanderbilt greeted him. She was an older woman who glittered with every motion she wore so many diamonds. "It's so nice to see you again. We've already donated, but I'm interested in doing more. Is there a foundation set up for these kids?"

Mia's heart fluttered. It was her dream to set up a foundation. The fact that someone was asking about it gave her hope that someday it could become a reality.

"Mia can tell you more," Ethan told her, motioning to Mia. "She's the star of the show tonight."

Mrs. Vanderbilt smiled warmly at her and Mia's smile grew.

"There's a couple of charities I can recommend," Mia said, slowly gaining confidence. "Your donation here goes a long way. Let me tell you about some of our kids..."

Ethan winked at her and Mia focused on telling the donors about her sweet Grayson and how they could help him and others like him. A fresh wave of optimism swept over her. This was going to be amazing. She was going to make sure a lot of kids got help tonight.

Chapter 24

*M*ia

NINE HOURS LATER, Mia's feet hurt so badly she could barely walk, but she didn't care. She barely felt it. She was on top of the world. She couldn't stop smiling, even though her face ached. She was fairly sure she wasn't going to stop smiling for at least the next week.

"I had a wonderful time with you tonight," Ethan told her as he walked her out of the theater. She held onto his arm less for stability and more because he was half carrying her. Mia and high heels were not friends.

"Thank you so much, Ethan," Mia told him. "I don't know how I would have done it without you. You sure know how to work a crowd."

Ethan grinned. "That's why Carter pays me the big bucks," he told her. "Here's your ride home."

He brought her to the side of a long black limo. The

street was quiet since everyone else had long ago gone home. Not even the bars were open anymore.

"Thank you again," she said as the driver came around to open the door for her. "And thank you for donating, too. It means the world to me."

He chuckled. "After listening to you rave about how amazing these kids are and how far even a dollar would go to help them, how could I not donate something?" He gave her hand a squeeze. "I had a great time. I'm actually glad I got to go to this, but don't tell Carter or he'll get all jealous."

She nodded. "Mum's the word, got it."

The driver opened the door, and Ethan helped her inside. "Have a wonderful night," he said as she slid inside.

"I will," she replied. She paused and grinned at him. "And I'll tell Laura you say hello."

Hope and fear filled his face at the same time, making him look like he was either going to be sick or start dancing in the street. She couldn't help but laugh a little as he quickly regained control and glared at her. There was definitely something going on between those two. She didn't know what, but she had a feeling she would find out eventually.

The driver shut the door, and Ethan shook his head as he walked away. Mia chuckled to herself and relaxed back against the seat, closing her eyes. Now that she was in a dark, quiet space, she was suddenly exhausted. Talking to hundreds of people was a lot of effort.

"I take it things went well?" a voice asked in the darkness. It was a voice that Mia knew and loved.

"Carter!" she exclaimed, opening her eyes. He was sitting near the driver, hidden from view of the door. "What are you doing here?"

"Making sure Ethan doesn't steal my girl," he replied.

"Do I have to go challenge him to a fight at noon by the flagpole?"

"He was a perfect gentleman," Mia assured him, sliding on the black leather seat to sit next to him. He held open his arm, and she leaned into him, instantly relaxed by his touch. "I think he's got eyes for someone else. You have no reason to be jealous."

"He got to spend all evening with you dressed like this," Carter replied, looking her over. "How can I not be jealous?"

"Because it was your idea?" Mia offered. She snuggled into him. "Besides, even if he had been interested, I'm not on the market."

Carter's arms tightened around her, and his chest swelled beneath her cheek. She smiled, knowing that her words made him happy.

"Tell me how it- hold on, I was supposed to get this call an hour ago." Carter pulled out his vibrating phone from his pocket. "Carter."

The voice on the other end said something, but Mia couldn't hear what it was.

"That's not negotiable," Carter informed whoever was on the phone. He listened for a moment, and his face hardened. A change came over him, and suddenly he was no longer the easy-going horse owner and car designer. His voice went cold and sharp as he transitioned into the billionaire businessman. "And what did you tell them?"

Mia sat with her head on his shoulder, trying not to eavesdrop. This was obviously a business call, and as she wasn't an employee, she didn't feel quite right about listening to it, but she didn't have much of a choice.

"That isn't an option," Carter said. "You have two choices here, either take my deal as is or don't. This isn't a negotiation."

The easy softness that she was used to hearing in his voice was gone. He was all business. Yet, he still cradled her against him with the utmost care. He was two people, as Mia realized most people were. The lover and the businessman. The lover and the fighter. The man and the money.

The person on the other end said something, but Mia was fighting to keep her eyelids open. Now that the party was over and she no longer had to be "on," she was exhausted. A full day of work in addition to working a party was more than she was built to handle.

"You've made the right choice," Carter said into the phone, his voice warm again. "We'll talk again tomorrow to work out all the details. Goodnight."

He clicked his phone off and carefully slid it into his pocket. With his hand now free, he brushed a strand of hair from her cheek with such gentle care it made her heart smile.

"Good phone call?" she asked, closing her eyes as he stroked her hair.

"Yes," he replied. "And how about you? How was the fundraiser?"

"Amazing." She stifled a yawn as she sat up to look at his face. "I can't thank you enough for this. Ethan thinks we raised over two million dollars for the foster charity tonight, and I can't tell you how much that means."

"It means two million dollars?" Carter shrugged.

She chuckled and settled back into her spot on his shoulder. "No, it means that these kids get some real opportunities. It's such a great place to start."

He gave her a gentle squeeze. "I'm so glad you're happy. It was a good fundraiser?"

"Carter, it was perfect." She sat up and kissed his cheek. "You truly outdid yourself. I don't know how you created such a perfect atmosphere and got all those people to come. It was more than I ever could have dreamed of. Thank you so much."

He smiled. "You're happy, so I'm happy. That's all I wanted."

"Deliriously happy," she assured him with a yawn.

"Here," he said, patting the spot on his shoulder for her to place her head. "You rest. I'll make sure you make it home safe and sound."

"That sounds good," Mia said, resting her head. Her eyelids were so heavy that she could barely keep them open. "Thank you so much for this, Carter. It gives me hope that maybe I can start my own non-profit."

"You would be amazing at that," he told her, smoothing her hair against her temple. She sighed with contentment.

"Someday," she murmured, enjoying the idea. She had this beautiful idea of opening up a camp to help foster kids, but until today, it didn't seem feasible. After today, she felt like she could do anything.

"You had a busy night," Carter told her. "Close your eyes and rest."

"Okay," she said with a jaw-cracking yawn. She nestled down into his shoulder. He pulled a jacket up over her shoulders to keep her warm. She didn't open her eyes, but the jacket was soft and smelled like him. He was so comfortable as a pillow that she was asleep before she knew it.

She dreamed she was dancing with Carter at the fundraiser. She wore her beautiful dress, and he was in his ranch jeans and t-shirt, but everyone was clapping and cheering as they danced. All of her foster kids were there, dancing along with them. They all had new shoes and backpacks and smiles as big as the sky. It was a beautiful dream.

As their dance ended, she woke up to him carrying her

into her apartment. She stirred long enough to realize where she was before falling back asleep in his arms as he took care of her and put her into bed. He took off her shoes and carefully pulled off her dress before tucking her under the sheets with a gentle kiss on her forehead. She fell back asleep and continued to dance with him in her dreams, dancing the magical night away with her prince charming until morning.

Chapter 25

THE SUN DIPPED behind the mountains, turning the world into dark shadows and twilight. A cold autumn wind rattled the trees, and in the distance, a coyote howled for a meal. Carter checked his watch for what must have been the fifth time in ten minutes. He looked out the window again, waiting for Mia's car to arrive, even though she wasn't supposed to be here for another five minutes.

He just couldn't wait to see her again. It had been just over a month since their trip to Vegas, but he still felt just like he did that first night: giddy excited. Even after a month of regular dates, sleepovers, and fantastic sex, she still made him breathless and impatient to have her.

No one had ever kept his interest for this long. He knew that meant something, but he tried not to think about it. He wasn't ready to confess his feelings for her or to tell her just how serious he wanted to get. The last thing he wanted to do was scare her off.

Besides, once the death threats were over, he would leave the ranch and go back to his regular life. For not the first time since having that realization, he almost wished for more threats to come. He shook himself, telling him to snap out of it. Even if he wasn't at the ranch, he could still be with her. He did own a private jet.

Still, he was keeping his feelings to himself for now. He was going to shower her with attention, but he didn't need to say the words. That wasn't his style anyway. He was much more about action than talking.

Finally, he saw her headlights drive up the road. He tried to school his face into something suave and sexy, but a happy smile kept popping up and ruining it. As she opened the door, he stopped trying. She knew the real him anyway. He didn't need to impress her.

She opened the door, and his jaw nearly dropped. He didn't know how she did it. She was stunning. She'd changed into a cute white sweater with a pair of dark jeans that made her curves look amazing. It didn't matter if she was wearing a ball gown or a t-shirt, she managed to make everything look sexy as hell. The only thing he liked better was seeing her in nothing at all.

"Hey," she said, closing the door behind her. Her cheeks were flushed with the cold, and the wind had blown her hair into her eyes. She smiled at him, and he felt his blood speed up.

He kissed her, tasting the cold on her skin and the heat in her body. She moaned softly as he dipped his tongue into her mouth. His hand curled around the back of her neck, pulling her into him as he tasted her sweetness. She tasted like heaven.

He had planned to wait until after dinner. He had planned to romance her. He had a fantastic meal ready to go, and candles and flowers, but as he kissed her, he knew he didn't want to wait. That he couldn't wait. She was just too irresistible to him.

He pulled back, crossing his arms and grabbing the hem of his shirt to pull it off over his head. He loved the way her eyes traveled his body like she was hungry and he was an all-you-can-eat buffet. He pulled at his zipper and hooked his thumbs in his pants. She licked her lips as he pulled them down.

"This wasn't quite the meal I was expecting, but I'll take it," she commented, her eyes dark with desire. She dropped to her knees in front of him.

"You sure?" he asked. His plan was to get her naked, but when she looked up at him from her knees, all coherent thought vanished. She was so damn beautiful and good. He didn't deserve to have her subservient before him.

She reached out and stroked the growing bulge in his boxers. "I want to," she told him, her voice husky with desire. "Please."

Carter wasn't one to say no to a lady, so he just nodded.

She reached out and touched him again, finally hooking her fingers into the waistband and tugging the fabric down. The air was cool against his skin, but everything else in his world was hot. She looked up at him again, leaning forward to give him one long lick from stem to stern.

He nearly lost it right there.

To have the most beautiful woman in the world pleasuring him simply because she wanted to was enough to make any man's dreams come true. That she was damn good at it had him convinced he had died and gone to heaven. Or that he was dreaming.

She looked up at him through her eyelashes as she guided him into her mouth. The heat and the pressure of her tongue drove him wild. Heat raced up his spine, and his thoughts turned to mush. He groaned, tangling his fingers in her soft hair as she worked her tongue along his length.

He pulled her hair gently away. He'd planned tonight as a way to spoil her, not to be spoiled. She pouted as he stepped back, her perfect lips in a downturn. All he could think about was having them wrapped around him again, but he shook his head.

"You have far too many clothes on," he told her. Her frown gave way to a small smile. He helped her stand, catching the hem of her sweater as she rose. With a smooth motion, he lifted it up and over her head, tossing the soft fabric to the side. She wore only a lacy bra underneath, and it had him panting as soon as he saw it.

He gently caressed the soft swells of her breasts, forcing himself to take his time. All he really wanted to do was pick her up and carry her caveman style into the bedroom and have his way with her. Hell, he didn't even need to go to the bedroom. All he wanted to was to fill her and hear her voice cry out his name.

His hands went to her hips. She'd already undone the button to her dark jeans and was inching them off. Inch by inch, smooth skin on long legs appeared. He stared, loving every centimeter of her being. She kicked off her jeans to join her sweater, standing before him in nothing but a matching lacy set of bra and panties.

"I thought you might like these," she said, tossing her hair behind her shoulder and watching his reaction. He felt his whole body twitch with desire and she grinned.

"I do," he promised. "But, I need to see what they look like on the floor, too."

She chuckled, low and deep. The sound went straight into his core, filling him with lust. He wanted to be a part of that chuckle, to feel it from the inside. He fought himself for patience, knowing it would only get better if he waited.

He put his mouth on her shoulder, gently sucking and moving his teeth against the smoothness of her. She tasted delicious. Salty and clean, with the scent of rose. "You are so beautiful, Mia," he murmured huskily.

From her shoulder, he moved down to her collarbone, to her breast. He teased her nipples for a moment before sliding down further, dropping to his knees to kiss her belly. He found her hipbone and pressed his mouth against it.

He looked up just in time to see her mouth open in surprise. He liked her mouth open like that, so he went back to kissing her hips.

"So beautiful," he whispered, spreading his hand against her low belly. He lowered his hand, tracing a squiggling line from her belly button south to the core of her.

She bucked against his hand, wanting more pressure. He made the light motion again, only giving her a teasing taste of what was to come. She whined, and he pressed his head against her thigh, watching what he was about to do.

With the softest of touches, he rubbed the pad of his thumb right where he knew she wanted it most. She cried out, arching her back and grabbing at his shoulders as he knelt before her. He slowly repeated the motion, barely flicking his thumb against her, knowing each stroke was beautiful torture.

"Carter," she gasped, her hips shaking in his hands.

"More?" he asked politely, looking up and waiting for a response.

"Hell yes!"

He slid a finger between her thighs, keeping his thumb

on her pleasure center. She was already wet for him, and it took everything he had not to push her to the ground and take her right there. He wanted to pleasure her. He wanted to make her come with his fingers first, and then he could make her come on him.

He pumped his fingers up and down, working his thumb in quick circles. Her entire body vibrated with energy waiting to be released in the form of pleasure. He wanted to be the cause of that pleasure. He went faster, working his fingers to make her come undone.

Her hands went to his head, her fingers tangled in his hair so that he had to look up at her.

"Carter, I want you in me," she whispered. "I want you to feel me explode around you."

There was no way he could say no to that. She dropped to her knees before laying back on the carpeted floor. He didn't hesitate, moving to place himself at her entrance.

They both gasped as he slid deep into her. She came undone.

Carter held his breath as sensation overwhelmed him. He thought about letting himself go and coming with her, but he wasn't ready for this to be over that quickly. He focused on her, watching her writhe beneath him as she lost herself to sensation.

She was the most beautiful creature he had ever seen. How had he gotten so lucky?

Carter braced himself with his forearms on either side of her face. Her eyes slowly flickered open as she came down off her orgasm. Warm, chocolate brown eyes enveloped him as he began to rock his hips back and forth. She moved in tandem with him, meeting him stroke for stroke like the perfect partner she was.

He loved the way she moved beneath him, rolling her

hips to meet him. She cried out with every thrust, begging for more. His body responded, pushing harder and deeper and the fire inside of him rising to a fever pitch.

His body started to shake. There was no stopping him now. He reached down, cupping her chin in his hand as he lost himself to the pleasure of her body. Her eyes opened wide, finding his as she followed him into bliss. Together, they rocked and cried out, passion and euphoria washing over them in uncountable waves.

They were both breathing hard as he braced his weight on his forearms above her. She smiled up at him with stars in her eyes, and he leaned down to tenderly kiss her. Lust was replaced with something much calmer, but far more powerful.

Mia reached up and stroked his cheek with her hand, her eyes gazing up at him with love. "That was pretty awesome," she murmured.

"I thought so too," he agreed, making her chuckle. "Are you ready for the main course?"

"If that was appetizers, I can't wait to see what dessert is," she replied. She looked up at him, and her pupils dilated.

"Just wait until you see the main course," he teased, dipping his head to kiss her nose. She chuckled, and he loved how he could feel the vibrations of her laugh ripple through him.

"I can't wait," she replied. Her beautiful face twisted into a frown. "Is something burning?"

"Dinner," he said, quickly untangling himself from her body. The loss of her around him was worse than being punched in the gut, yet he knew he had to save their meal.

Running naked into the kitchen, he quickly pulled out the chicken breasts he'd put in to warm. He set them on the stove top, checking them to make sure they weren't too badly cooked.

"I was always told it was a bad idea to cook naked," Mia remarked, following him in. She didn't put on any clothes and the urge to take her again, this time on the kitchen table was strong.

"But I did save dinner," he said, pointing to his almost perfect chicken breast meal.

She grinned and took a deep inhale in. "It smells amazing," she said. "Did you make it yourself?"

"Of course I did," he said. Her eyebrows raised and he shrugged. "Okay, I didn't. I just heated it up. But, it should be delicious. I may not cook, but I can reheat like a total pro."

"I can't wait," she said, leaning up against one of the counters. His eyes followed her curves, his mouth craving her again already.

"It should cool in a minute," he said, his eyes going to the soft curve of her hip and the swell of her breast. He could feel himself stirring again already.

She bit her lip and grinned. "Like I said, if that was appetizers..." She licked her top lip, the pink of her tongue driving him wild. "I could go for the main course. You did promise something amazing."

He grinned. He made sure the oven was off and kissed her, pressing her naked skin into his right there in the kitchen. He wasn't about to tell her no, not when she looked absolutely edible. The chicken would taste just fine cold.

Chapter 26

$\mathcal{M}$ia

MIA SAT at the kitchen table of the ranch house, sipping hot chocolate and watching the clouds dance across the mountains. It was a cold, gray late October day where the sky kept threatening rain or snow but never delivering. She didn't feel well, so she was taking it easy while the kids worked in the barn. She hoped she wasn't coming down with a cold or the flu, but she'd never felt this tired in her life. She had never realized just how much energy it took to breathe before.

Carter waved to her from the front yard as he came in from the garage. She smiled and felt her heart warm. She still couldn't believe how successful the fundraiser he'd given her was. They'd raised more than she'd ever dreamed possible and it was making her rethink her dream of starting a foundation. If she could plan another fundraiser like that one, her own foundation to help foster kids wasn't such a pipe dream.

The door to the kitchen opened with a blast of frigid air. Carter stomped his feet outside and came in out of the cold. His cheeks were rosy with the cold, and his eyes sparkled. He came over and kissed the top of her head.

"You feeling okay? Laura was wondering where you were today," he asked, going to the kitchen and getting a glass of water.

Mia shrugged. "I'll live," she replied. She could see Laura running in and out of the barn as hay bales were brought in for the horses. There was a lot of hay. "How's Laura doing today? I know she had a rough night with her siblings the other day."

Carter took a sip of coffee and followed her gaze out the window.

"Better. She's still adjusting to becoming a parent," he replied. "She went from being a sister to a parent overnight, and none of them are used to it yet. I'm just glad she's back."

"Having something to do always helps," Mia agreed. She made a mental note to check in with Laura more. Suddenly becoming the legal guardian to her two younger siblings wasn't an easy thing. She could probably use a friend.

"She says that Lily's been amazing, though." Carter took another sip of water, finishing off his glass.

"Yeah?" Mia smiled.

"Laura told me she came back to find everything exactly how she wanted it. All she had to do was the things she hadn't taught Lily how to do yet," Carter told her, coming to stand next to her chair. "She can't say enough good things about Lily."

"I'm so glad," Mia said. "Lily has been working so hard to

make sure everything's perfect. I'm glad she can go back to focusing on school again. Her teachers were starting to complain that all she wrote for her essays was horse related."

Carter nodded and stared at the window at the gray afternoon.

"I never want kids," he said out of nowhere.

Mia spun in her chair to look at him.

"What makes you say that?" she asked.

"I don't think I could handle the responsibility," he said quietly. His blue eyes kept looking out the window, his face drawn and serious as he watched Laura struggle with an unruly bale of hay.

Mia snorted and gave his hip a gentle push. "You can handle a billion-dollar company, thousands of jobs, and you run a ranch. You literally can snap your fingers and completely change someone's life, but kids are too big a responsibility?"

"I don't actually handle my company, Ethan does. But, well, when you say it that way, it sounds silly," he acknowledged. He looked at her. "But, look at Laura. Anything can happen, and kids complicate things. They make every decision different."

"You know, that's not necessarily a bad thing," she replied.

"Don't get me wrong, I like kids. Grayson, Alexander, and Lily are amazing," he said.

"But?"

"But I'm not cut out to be a parent." He set his empty glass down on the table and sighed. "Have you seen my hours? It's not fair to anyone for me to have kids. Plus, I have death threats. I couldn't risk what happened to Laura's family."

Mia nodded, staying quiet. She already knew he didn't

want kids, but hearing him actually say the words made her sad. It was a moot point though.

I can't have kids anyway, she thought to herself. *I guess that makes us the perfect couple.*

Carter's phone chirped loudly, making her jump.

"Sorry, I have it on extra loud since I was in the garage," Carter apologized. He read the message and smiled. "Brian thinks he has a lead on my security issues."

"That's great!" Mia told him. "I can't believe he's evaded the police this long. I thought you said the threats died down after the fundraiser?"

"They did," he replied, tucking the phone back in his pocket. "But, he thinks he has a new lead. I'm going to go see what he's got."

"Okay." Mia smiled and looked at her cup of hot chocolate. All she wanted was a nap.

"You still up for dinner tonight?" he asked, heading back to the door.

She smiled and nodded. "Dinner sounds great."

He smiled at her and headed out with a blast of cold air, waving at her as he passed the window. She chuckled, feeling lucky for a moment, but once he was gone from her sight, the gray melancholy of the day came back over her.

"Why am I feeling so down?" she asked herself. She tried to go through reasons in her head. No one else in the office was sick. It could be the weather. She'd been eating better recently, so it wasn't that. Maybe it was her time of the month? She pulled out her phone and checked her calendar. She was technically a week late at this point, but she'd never been "regular" in her life, so it wasn't that strange.

She frowned and then shrugged. She probably was just going to start her period soon. That would explain the tiredness. That or she was simply catching the flu. She really hoped it was just her period.

One of the security guards walked past the window. She knew this one's name since he usually greeted the kids on their way in. His name was Ben. He seemed nice enough, but there was something sad to him that Mia couldn't put her finger on. He seemed always to be working. She did know that he genuinely seemed protective of the kids, which she appreciated.

He nodded to her as he passed the window and she raised her hand in greeting. It felt like it would take too much energy to do a full wave. He kept going, his face serious as he patrolled the ranch. She watched him for a moment, glad that there were people keeping Carter safe. She hoped Brian's lead was solid. She wanted Carter to be free of these threats.

Chapter 27

$\mathcal{M}$ia

MIA DROVE while the kids rested from their long day in court. Grayson was snoring softly in his booster seat while Lily and Alexander stared out their window at the passing cars. Everyone was quiet and pensive.

After the hearing, Mia took the kids so that Margie could stay in the city and do some shopping. It was an easy thing to do since she was supposed to take the kids to the ranch that afternoon anyway. They just had to head to their foster house and change before heading out. Mia was looking forward to seeing Carter. Seeing him would brighten her day, and she needed it.

The afternoon spent in court was a standard six-month hearing, but it still took a lot of energy. The hearing had been uneventful. Nothing was changing, although the judge wasn't happy with the fact that Margie the foster mom had been "retired" out of the system for so long. While there wasn't a problem currently, it made Mia uneasy about the kids' future with her. If anything happened, it would be the kids that would suffer.

Mia sighed as she turned off the highway. There was nothing she could do to make this situation better. Margie was their best option right now, especially given the kids' turbulent history. She was so glad that working at the ranch was making their behavior better, but it was still a tenuous existence. If anything happened, the three siblings would be split up and sent to different foster homes.

Mia glanced around at the kids. They needed one another. They were a family and splitting them up, no matter how much sense it made on paper, would be the wrong thing for all of them. There was so much potential in them that she wished there was something more she could do, but she'd already gone above and beyond.

She wished that she could just adopt all three of them. She would if she could, but she knew she couldn't afford three kids on her social worker salary. Not that they'd even give them to her. She shook her head and tried not to think about it. She was getting too attached to this little family, and she knew it, but she didn't care. These kids were special to her.

Mia pulled into the subdivision where the kids lived and up to Margie's house. A cloud passed over the quiet neighborhood, and the hairs on Mia's arms stood on end. Something was wrong. She knew it the moment she pulled onto the street.

"Stay in the car," she told the kids, putting the car in park along the sidewalk and opening her door. She stayed in the doorway of the car where she knew it was safe, staring at the house.

The front window into the living room was smashed

open. The curtains billowed out of the house in the fall wind. The white curtains were almost pretty against the dark brick, if not for the broken glass and graffiti. Spray-painted across the white garage door in blood red paint were the words, "DON'T LET HIM KILL THEM TOO."

Mia's hands shook as she grabbed her cell phone and quickly dialed 911.

"There's been a break-in," she told the operator. She was surprised that her voice wasn't shaking. She wasn't used to calling 911, and it felt strange. "I'm going to need an officer."

"Are you in immediate danger?" asked the operator.

Mia shook her head as she replied even though she was on the phone. "No, I don't think so."

"Stay in your car, and we'll send an officer as soon as possible," the operator assured her. The calm voice on the other end then asked her some questions and took her information. With nothing left to talk about until the police officer showed up, Mia hung up the phone and sat in the driver's seat.

Mia took a deep breath and re-read the words on the door. The "he" had to mean Carter. She knew it in her bones. Everyone liked Margie, and there was no way Alexander or Grayson had killed anyone. But, if someone wanted to get to Carter, this was as good a way as any. Whoever was after him had upgraded their harassment to include her and the kids simply because they spent time with him.

"Mia?" Lily's voice was low and afraid. "What does that mean?"

Mia let out a shaky breath and tried to put on her most confident smile. She patted Lily's hand. "Don't let it scare you. It's not meant for you."

"Okay," Lily replied, but it was obvious she didn't really

believe Mia. In the backseat, Alexander was hunkered down in his seat and frowning. At least Grayson was still asleep and oblivious to what was going on.

Mia picked up her cell phone again. She dialed the number she now knew by heart.

"This is Carter," he answered, sounding professional and a little bit busy.

"Carter, it's Mia." She felt stupid, but she wasn't quite sure how to start this conversation.

"How are you?" His voice was instantly warmer, and she could hear the smile in his voice.

"I already called the cops, but I thought you should know. The person sending you those threats sent one to the kids' house," she blurted out. She grimaced slightly, knowing there was probably a better way to put it.

"What did they do?" The warmness was gone. His voice was cold and with a hum of anger to it.

"They broke a window and spray painted 'don't let him kill them too' on the garage," she explained. "I can't see any other damage from out here."

"I'm sending over a security team. Don't go in the house. Stay in your car until they get there." Mia had never heard him speak so forcibly before. He was kind of scary.

"Okay," she promised. "That's what we were planning on doing anyway."

"Good. Heads will roll for this." He slammed something down on a table wherever he was. "Someone will be there in five minutes. Stay safe."

"We will," she told him. He hung up on her to call his security team and she carefully pocketed her phone. She checked her watch to see only a couple of minutes had passed. Hopefully, the police would be here soon.

"What's going on Mia?" Lily asked, more insistent this time.

Mia chewed on the inside of her cheek for a moment before turning to face the three of them. Grayson had woken up and was looking around confused at why they were still in the car.

"I'm sure it's just some kind of prank, but I'm just being careful," Mia explained.

"Why'd you call Carter? And what do you mean he's been getting threats?" Lily asked, her eyes narrowing slightly. Alexander crossed his arms and waited for an answer.

"I called Carter because he has resources to help us," Mia said. "As for the threats, Carter owns a very successful business. People get angry with him, and they threaten him. That's why he has so much security around his house. It happens a lot to important people."

"Kind of like the president and the secret service?" Grayson asked, tilting his head.

"Exactly like the president," Mia agreed with a smile.

"Is that Ben?" Lily asked, pointing to a man walking toward them. "He's one of the security guards at the ranch. He's always nice."

Mia had been so busy talking to the children that she hadn't seen the black truck pull up on the opposite side of the street. She checked her watch, amazed that Ben had beaten the cops.

Ben walked confidently over to Mia's window. He wore jeans and a W motors t-shirt, rather than the usual dark security uniform. She could see that he was carrying a weapon in the waistband of his pants, and she wondered just how serious this was. Mia rolled down her window to talk to him.

"Are you four okay?" he asked, looking into the car with a frown.

"Yeah, we're just waiting on the police," Mia replied. "How did you get here so quickly? There's no way you came from the ranch."

"I was just driving in for the night-shift. Cards called me since he knew this is on my way into work," Ben explained. "He's on his way as well, but he wanted someone here to make sure you and the kids were taken care of."

His story made complete sense to Mia, and she smiled at him. She still felt on edge and off-centered, but she was glad he was there. Besides, she liked Ben. He was always good with the kids.

"Thank you, Ben," Mia told him. "We're doing okay. Just creeped out."

"I'll stay with you until the police arrive," Ben told her. "Then we'll get to the bottom of this."

"WE DIDN'T FIND any sign of the intruder, ma'am," the police officer told her. She stood on the front porch of Margie's house with police lights flashing everywhere. She was fairly sure the neighbors were going to accidentally rip the blinds off their windows if they kept peeking out like they were.

Mia nodded. She could see Brian and Ben talking with two other police officers by the garage. A crime scene camera flashed for what felt like the millionth time at the garage. She turned back to what the head officer was telling her.

"The window was broken in with a rock from the yard. We've cleared the house and made sure that no one is inside or anywhere on the property. We made sure they didn't leave any surprises behind in the house," the officer was saying. "Whoever did this isn't here anymore."

"Thank you, officer," Mia replied, nodding along. She still felt weirded out by it all though and wasn't looking forward to going to her own empty apartment. Maybe she could get Brian to check it out before he went into work. It would certainly make her feel better.

"If you have any other trouble, be sure to let us know." The officer put his pen and pad back into his pocket. "We'll finish up and get out of your hair, ma'am."

"Thank you again, Officer."

The police officer turned and went down the stairs of the porch as Brian Cards came up them. Even compared to the police officer, the man was huge. She felt safer with him around and was glad Carter had sent him. He'd arrived just shortly after the police.

"I'm going to have a man patrolling outside the house tonight," Brian told her. "Tomorrow, Mr. Williamson is having a security system installed here and at your apartment with twenty-four-hour monitoring. This isn't happening again."

He definitely reminded her of a bear protecting its cubs. She was glad she was one of those cubs because the man was fierce. She nodded and took a deep breath in, trying to calm herself. She could see Margie in the car with the kids. The overhead light was on, and she suspected Margie had them working on homework. Their trip to the ranch was obviously not happening now.

Brian put his big hand on her shoulder. She could feel the strength in it and was glad he was on her side. Ben came up the stairs with a large piece of plywood and a hammer, and Brian gave her a gentle squeeze before going to help him with it. Together, the two men started boarding up the broken window as Mia watched.

"I'd say that looks familiar, but the joke feels a little dark," Carter said from behind her. His voice was exactly what she wanted to hear.

"Maybe it was just two boys trying to show off for their friends?" she joked, as she turned and smiled at him. "I'm pretty sure Margie's bowling trophies are pretty valuable."

As soon as he was up the short walkway, he put his arms around her and kissed her temple. She relaxed into him, feeling her anxiety lessen as soon as he touched her.

"I'm sorry I put you in this situation," he said softly, still holding her close. She pushed him away gently so she could look up at him. His blue eyes were full of concern, and his brow was dark.

"You didn't put me in this situation," she told him. She motioned to the nearly boarded up window. "Whoever did this is a horrible person. Scaring kids to get revenge? They suck. Not you."

He smiled and hugged her again. "I'm just glad you and the kids are safe."

"Me too," she agreed. She looked over at the now ugly window and frowned. "I get why you were so mad about your window now."

Carter chuckled, and she was glad to see his face relax slightly. "Plus, the heating bill increases are insane."

She smiled and leaned against him. The hammer against the plywood echoed through the neighborhood, and she shivered. The sun had gone down and now the night air was chilly.

"I'm just glad no one was home," Mia said softly.

"I don't want you or the kids staying here tonight," he told her. "Or at your apartment."

"They sent officers over to check it out," Mia informed him. "They didn't find anything there."

"I don't care," he replied. "You, the kids, and even Margie aren't staying here."

"So where are we staying?" she asked, already knowing the answer. The man had a big beautiful ranch with no one but him living on it.

"With me."

Mia loved the way he said it. There was warmth and protection in his voice, and his embrace around her shoulders tightened. There was no way he was going to let anything happen to any of them.

"The kids would love a slumber party," she told him. "They still talk about being able to sleep in the barn."

Carter chuckled. "I have someplace better than the barn for them. I had some rooms made up for them."

Mia smiled up at him. He grinned and pulled her away from the broken window and over to where the kids sat in the car. Despite his fame and fortune, he really was a big sweetheart. She suspected he liked the kids far more than he let on.

THE KIDS PILED out of the SUV with their overnight bags and giggled as they raced across the dead lawn to the ranch house. Behind them, Carter helped Mia carry her bag as well as the excess kid stuff as they followed behind. Margie had opted to spend the night at a friend's house, which Carter said was fine.

Once inside the house, Carter took the lead.

"Follow me," he told the kids, leading them down the hallway and toward the basement door. Mia frowned but followed along. She remembered the basement as finished, but full of old computers and random equipment. Carter hadn't done anything to it yet since he was only here until the threats ended. She had assumed they would sleep on the couches in the living room for the night.

Carter grinned at her, his eyes twinkling with the light of a secret as he opened the basement door. The kids rushed down in front of him with Mia trailing behind. She gasped as she came down the steps and saw the transformation that Carter had made to the basement.

Instead of a regular basement, it looked like a house. There was a common area with three distinct bedrooms coming off of it. From just the open doorways, Mia could see that each room was fully decorated and furnished.

"When you said you had rooms made up for them, I assumed you bought some air mattresses and extra sheets," Mia told him, standing in the common room and looking around.

"Right. Because billionaires buy air mattresses," he replied. She looked up at him, and he winked at her.

She shook her head and went to see what each room contained. It was far more than just a mattress in each room. Each room was clearly designed for one of her kids.

The pale yellow room with turquoise accents was made for Lily. There were books about horses and other animals on the beautiful white wood nightstand. It was pretty and feminine, yet strong and elegant enough to suit a teenager. Lily already had her nose in a book about equine anatomy as she lounged on the bed.

Alexander's room was done in shades of blue and orange, with sports equipment and several signed football jerseys decorating the walls. Alexander sat on the foot of his football themed bedspread with a deliriously happy look on his face as he stared at the wall with the jerseys of his heroes.

Mia left him to find Grayson pretending to drive his race car bed around the room. The youngest boy's room was painted to look like a racing stadium. Painted crowds cheered as Grayson made engine noises and shifted a pillow gear shift.

"You outdid yourself," Mia told Carter as she came back to the common room. She couldn't believe how amazing this all was. Even the common room was made for comfort. There was a large leather couch and a big screen TV. "I can't believe you did all this."

Carter shrugged. "I was thinking about it the other day. I'm planning on having more foals, and the hay wasn't that comfortable," he explained. "This way, they have a place to stay."

"Just for foaling?" Mia asked, raising an eyebrow at him.

"Yeah." He shrugged as if the complete home makeover was nothing more than getting a couple of extra pillows for the couches.

She went to her tiptoes and kissed his cheek. "I think those kids might be growing on you."

He chuckled. "Maybe a little."

With a smile, he took her hand and together they went to tuck the kids into bed for the evening. Although, given how excited they all were, Mia doubted they were ever going to go to sleep.

Chapter 28

Mia

MIA KISSED Grayson's forehead as his eyelids fluttered shut in the dim light of his nightlight. Even his nightlight was race-car themed with the light coming out of a pair of headlights on the wall. She carefully closed the door and stepped into the common room. The other two were tucked in bed with books and heavy eyelids that didn't look like they were going to last long.

Mia thought that the kids were going to stay up all night, enjoying their new rooms. It was the first time they'd each had their own room, let alone a room decorated to suit their preferences, and Mia has figured they'd be living it up.

However, the events of the day had worn them out. It was a testament to how well Carter had crafted each room that the kids all fell asleep in less than thirty minutes once teeth were brushed and pajamas on. The kids felt like they were at home and fell asleep with ease.

"Well, that was easier than I expected," Carter announced as they slipped upstairs to the living room. "And they say parenting is hard."

Mia laughed. Then they both held their breath as they waited for one of the kids to prove them wrong. After a statement like that, it was practically inevitable that one of them would call up the stairs needing a glass of water or needing just one more hug.

Nothing came, and slowly they let out their lungs.

"No more jinxing things," Mia whispered. She gave him a gentle punch to his arm.

"How about a drink?" Carter offered.

"I'd actually love a cup of cocoa," Mia admitted. "Your machine makes the best I've ever had."

"The best you've ever had, huh?" Carter winked. "Do I need to pick up some pointers?"

"Be made of melted chocolate?" Mia offered. "You're already hot."

Her compliment made him laugh as they walked to the kitchen. From there, Carter went to the cabinets and pulled out the cups and prepped the espresso machine with the cocoa pods. It hummed to life, frothing milk and heating the water.

It wasn't long before Carter handed her a steaming mug of perfect hot chocolate. She took in a deep sniff and let out a ragged sigh of pleasure as she took a sip.

"That's basically orgasmic," she said, taking a deeper and longer sip.

"Keep that up, and I'm going to get jealous," Carter remarked. He was watching her drink with laughter in his eyes.

"Jealous, huh?" Mia looked up at him and innocently batted her eyelashes before taking another sip. This time, she made a show of it. Closing her eyes, she drank deeply, then moaned low and ragged. Her back arched, pushing out her chest and she bit her lip before opening her eyes to look at Carter.

Carter's pupils dilated, turning his eyes into deep pools of desire. Mia's core flashed hot, and it wasn't from drinking the cocoa. Lust fluttered in her stomach, quickly flying south and heating everything on the way.

"And what are you going to do about it?" Mia asked, her voice going husky.

Her temperature only increased as Carter stepped next to her, putting his lips next to her ear.

"First, I'll take you away from the bad influences of this drink," Carter whispered, tracing a finger down her shoulder. "Then, I'll take you upstairs and show you just what I've got that your little chocolate drink can't compete with."

Mia shivered. She set the mug down, her thoughts no longer on the chocolate.

"Show me," she whispered. The lust in his eyes made her breath come in short gasps.

The corner of his mouth turned up in a cocky smile. He held out his hand for her to take. She stood up, the drink completely forgotten at this point. The only thing on her mind now was getting to a room with a door and a lock. The kids could get their own damn water.

Together, they tiptoed past the basement stairs, straining their ears for any sound before hurrying up to the bedroom. Carter led with big, confident steps that were just fast enough to keep Mia from getting frustrated and running ahead of him.

Once in the bedroom, Mia turned and shut the door, carefully locking it behind her. This was going to be way better than any chocolate drink.

The two of them threw themselves at each other, kissing furiously. His hands were all over her, from her hair to her back to her sides to her ass, touching every part they could. The callouses on his hands from working with cars and horses caressed her, giving extra sensation to every touch.

He grabbed her hips, pulling her into him with strong fingers. She wrapped her arms around his shoulders, tangling fingers in his hair as they stumbled towards the bed. She giggled, feeling like they were sneaking off from their duties to make out. It made her feel like a naughty teenager, hiding from her parents.

They paused at the edge of the mattress, giggling and panting. Carter put both his hands on her cheeks, his eyes soaking in the features of her face. She felt beautiful when he looked at her like that. From the look in his eyes, she was the most beautiful woman he'd ever seen. He kissed her again, proving his point.

His hands went back down to her hips, and his fingers began to pull upward, bunching her silk shirt up and baring her skin. With every stroke of his finger against her hip, she felt shivers up her spine. His hands shifted to undo the button on her jeans. She reached down and wiggled out of them before he even had the chance to struggle with it.

He licked his lips, looking over her with nothing but her shirt and panties on.

"Still jealous of the hot chocolate?" Mia teased, making sure to give him the best angle to look at her.

"I think I've got the chocolate beat," he replied, his voice rough with desire. It heated Mia's blood.

He kissed her again, spinning her around before pushing her onto the bed. Her body was on the edge of the bed with her knees bent and feet on the floor. Mia relaxed back, as he looked her over. He growled, low and appreciative before going to his knees before her. Mia tensed for a moment, then forced herself to relax as he positioned himself between her open knees. This was going to be good.

His fingers hooked the edges of her underwear and pulled down, revealing her to him. He let out a low moan of desire, and she nearly came just from the sound. He wanted her, and only her.

He leaned forward and kissed her where her legs joined. This time, it was Mia that let out the groan of desire. Carter didn't hesitate. He put his tongue to work, teasing her and pleasuring her with every lick.

His fingers joined his mouth. He used them to discover every inch, every pleasurable inch of her body until she was undulating, her fingers white-knuckling their grip on the bed. Her eyes closed, and she lost herself to his touch.

"Definitely better than chocolate," Mia gasped once she could breathe again. Carter looked up at her with a pleased smirk.

"All chocolate, or just cocoa?" he asked, rocking back on his heels and watching her come down from her orgasm.

"You might have to show me again," Mia replied. "You've got cocoa beat, but all chocolate?"

Carter chuckled and stood, putting his knees on either side of her hips on the bed. He still had his jeans and t-shirt on, but it was very obvious that he was enjoying this.

"You have too many clothes on," Mia complained, her hands going to his belt and jean button. He chuckled, taking off his shirt as she worked on freeing him from his pants. He stood up again, kicking his pants to the side and tossing his shirt to join them. All he was left wearing was a pair of boxers that were straining to contain him.

"Now you've got too many clothes on," Carter replied. He reached down and splayed his hands on her bare stomach, slowly moving them up and taking the shirt with them. She raised her head and arms, and he pulled the silk shirt from her, tossing it to join his clothing.

"Now we're even," she whispered, looking up at him. Good lord, did she want him. Every fiber of her being called out to have him within her. She needed him to be a part of her, to touch her and become one with her. She didn't want to wait, no matter how much fun waiting was.

Carter ran his hand over the tips of her bra, making her nipples react under the soft satin. Mia quickly sat up and undid the bra, tossing it to join the rest of the clothing.

"Now you're winning," Carter whispered. He leaned down, taking a nipple into his mouth and sucking. His hand went to the other breast to give it attention too.

"Hurry and catch up, then," Mia replied, arching her back. Her words ended in a moan as he flicked his tongue against her nipple, sending a rush of pleasure down her spine. His hand let go of her breast, and he used it to wiggle free of his boxers. At last, they were both naked.

The heat from his skin was heavenly. His chest pressed against her stomach, his mouth still working a nipple, and the body heat was better than a warm blanket.

"Chocolate might be winning," Mia whispered, reaching down and stroking his manhood. She didn't want to wait anymore. She wanted him now.

He chuckled as let go of her breast, fisting a hand in her hair, he pulled her head back to kiss her. His hand gripped her hip to hold her right where he wanted her. "Is that so?" he whispered.

His erection throbbed against her thigh, the heat of him coursing through her. His need mirrored her own, as she buried her nose into the curve of his shoulder. He smelled so good, the clean scent of hay and the outdoors filling her nose. How was it possible for a man to smell so damn good?

"Mia," he groaned, burying himself into her. The sudden completion made her gasp and writhe beneath him. How could she ever go back to being the way she was? How could she ever live without his touch again? She needed him in her like the desert needed the rain.

She reached up, stretching to kiss him and bring her lips to his. He dipped his head, kissing her as he rolled his hips, filling her yet again and again. His hands went to hers, pinning them beside her head as he worked his hips in a languid loop, filling her over and over again.

She lost her mind to the pleasure. He completed her so perfectly that she couldn't imagine ever feeling this incredible. Then he shifted his weight, going deeper inside of her, and she decided *that* was the most amazing feeling.

Skin pressed to skin, their pace quickened. Frantic need began to overtake slow desire. Her body arched and writhed to meet him, wanting him to fill her even deeper. His strength filled her, pushing her pleasure higher and higher with every thrust.

What he had done with his tongue earlier had been spectacular. This blew that out of the water. She shattered completely, Carter's name on her lips as she ascended into ecstasy.

This was so much more than just physical release. It was a merging of souls. Carter and Mia, they were meant to be together, and Mia could feel it with every atom of her being. They were made for one another.

Carter groaned, his breaths coming quick and ragged. Her orgasm was fueling his, sending him up and over the top of pleasure. She reached up her hand to his cheek as she smiled.

"Come for me, Carter," she whispered. "I want you."

"Mia..." His body stilled, tensing and trembling as he lost all his senses. She loved the way his eyes dilated, the way that he held her to him like she was the most precious thing he had ever known. Even with his mind lost to pleasure, he was aware of her.

Mia melted into him, absorbing everything about him. His heat filled her, and she whispered his name. She rocked her hips, taking every inch of him that she could. He gasped her name again, whispering it as he fell forward, covering her body with his own.

She held him to her, her fingers tracing designs along his beautiful muscular back. His weight felt right against her, holding her to this earth and keeping her content. If he wasn't there, she was so happy she felt like she might float off like a helium balloon.

Carter nuzzled her shoulder, giving her soft kisses and humming into her skin. She was deliriously happy for no other reason than she was with him. How was it possible for someone to make another person feel so complete?

"How was that?" Carter asked, his voice muffled by her shoulder. She chuckled, still coming down off her orgasm.

"Okay," she said after a while. "You beat chocolate."

Chapter 29

M *ia*

MIA WALKED down the aisles of the grocery store humming softly to herself. It was the first time in what felt like weeks that she'd had a moment to spend on herself and get to the grocery store. She was nearly out of food, but luckily, the only thing that sounded good lately was cereal, so she wasn't in too bad of shape. However, she'd run out of toothpaste this morning and was now at the store on her lunch break. She could deal with cereal for every meal, but she wanted to have nice breath when she kissed Carter.

She wandered through the pharmacy, picking up some antacids. Her stomach had been a little queasy the night before, so she wanted to stock up. As she passed through the aisles, she came to the feminine hygiene aisle.

The aisle was relatively unmarked, but there was a half empty stand of chocolate bars on the end-cap, so someone knew what they were doing. She chuckled to herself and tried to remember if she needed to pick up more supplies for herself. She did the mental math, trying to remember if she'd bought a new box of tampons last cycle, or the one before.

She nearly dropped her basket of groceries as she realized she was well over two weeks late. She'd completely forgotten about it. While never exactly regular, she had only ever been this late in a cycle once in her life. It was when she'd miscarried and found out that she would never have kids.

With worried hands, Mia grabbed the cheapest pregnancy test and tossed it in her basket. Suddenly, she didn't feel like wandering the aisles anymore, so she hurried to the self-checkout lane and quickly scanned everything. She tried not to blush as she scanned her pregnancy test, but no one was watching anyway.

Outside the sun was shining, but it was colder than Mia expected. Mia shivered against the sudden temperature change. Winter was coming, but it was still fall for now. She tried to make herself excited for Halloween and Pumpkin Spice lattes as she walked to her car, but the small blue and pink box in her bag had hold of her thoughts.

The drive back to her office was uneventful, yet it seemed to take forever. She made it back with five minutes still left on her lunch. Even if she'd been hungry, the thought of taking the test was more powerful than the pull of food. She ducked into the employee bathroom and went to her favorite stall.

She sent a silent thank you up to the heavens that the bathroom was empty as she opened the box and pulled out the plastic stick. She followed the instructions, her heart in her throat as she finished and set it down to dry.

She leaned against the stall door, feeling a little silly. It was probably nothing. The doctor told her that she would never get pregnant. She probably just wasted a nice latte's worth of money on a test she didn't need. Her body probably just skipped a cycle due to stress or something.

The timer on her phone went off indicating that it was time to check the results. Her hands shook slightly, and she tried to ignore her nerves. She picked up the box and reread the directions just to make sure she was doing this right: two lines meant she was pregnant and one meant she was just being silly.

She set down the box and picked up the pee stick. Two pink lines filled the square. Mia blinked twice and re-checked the box. She reread it three more times, comparing the picture on the box to the test just to make sure. She wished she'd splurged and gotten the one that spelled out clearly "YOU'RE PREGNANT" instead of the cheap one that just had lines.

Two lines meant pregnant. She stared at those two lines for a moment, unsure if she was excited, scared, upset, or worried. Probably all of the above, she decided.

There was a chance that it was a false positive. The doctors had told her that she would never conceive, yet here was a positive test. She didn't want to hope if it wasn't true.

She picked up her phone and quickly dialed her OBGYN. Upon explaining her situation and history, she was able to get an emergency appointment later that day. Her boss would be okay with letting her out a little early, especially if it was for a doctor's appointment. Given how much the fundraiser had raised, her boss was willing to let her do just about anything.

With shaking hands, Mia put the test in the box and put that in her purse. She felt a little weird saving something she'd peed on, but she wasn't sure if the doctor would want to see it, so she was keeping it. Besides, it was the only thing that told her this was real.

Mia let out a long breath and tried to figure out how she was going to get any work done until her appointment.

THE PAPER of her gown crinkled as she tried to find a comfortable position on the cold plastic of the exam table. The back of the exam table either needed to be up just a little bit higher so she could lean against it, or flatter so she didn't feel like she could lean. There was no comfortable way to sit, but the table wasn't long enough to lay down on without putting her feet up in the stirrups. Add in that the paper gown let in a draft and left her back exposed, and it wasn't a very comfortable position to be in.

"I'm sorry to keep you waiting," the doctor told her as she entered the physician's side door pulling a machine behind her. Dr. Misti-Cooper had a friendly smile and an easy manner that helped Mia feel more comfortable.

"Did you get the results?" Mia asked. She fiddled with the string of the gown between her fingers. Half of her wanted a yes and the other a no. She wasn't ready to be pregnant, but then again, she'd never thought that it would ever happen.

The doctor sat on the small rolling chair and scooted over to take her hand. "The test came back positive," she told her.

Mia gasped and couldn't help the tears that filled her eyes. The doctor gave her a moment, just holding her hand and being a solid presence.

"You okay?" Dr. Misti-Cooper asked. "I'm guessing this was rather unexpected."

"Very unexpected," Mia told her. "What happens next?"

"Well, given your history, we need to check the placement of the embryo with an ultrasound." The doctor smiled and pulled the ultra sound machine over. "It won't hurt at all."

Mia nodded. She was having a hard time staying calm. There was so much that could go wrong. What if she was pregnant, but the baby was in the wrong spot? What if the test the doctor did was actually wrong and there was nothing there? What if the test showed she was just going to lose this pregnancy too?

She'd given up on the idea that she would ever be a mother to her own biological children. The thought that she had a chance was terrifying and exciting. She just hoped she wasn't going to be let down and have to go through the process of knowing she'd never have this opportunity ever again.

"Lay back and relax," Dr. Misti-Cooper told her, booting up the machine and getting some gel out. "This is going to feel a little odd."

Mia nodded as the doctor got the ultrasound wand prepped. "I'm ready."

"Okay. Cold and pressure," the doctor said. Mia tensed slightly but made herself breathe through it. She took a deep breath in, focusing on relaxing all her muscles and trying to hold still at the same time.

"You're doing great," Dr. Misti-Cooper told her, moving the wand around slightly. Mia could see the screen. It reminded her of an old black and white TV as strange shapes danced across the screen. "There he is."

On the screen was a little black spot on a white dot. It was different than the rest of the screen, and Mia instinctively knew it was her baby. A tear of pure joy welled up in her eyes, and she let out the breath she'd been holding in.

There was a baby.

"It won't look like a baby for a few more weeks," the doctor explained. She moved the computer mouse and started taking measurements. "But he's there. You're measuring at four weeks, three days and the placement is perfect."

Mia stared at that small dot on the screen. Emotions rolled through her in waves like the ocean, threatening to drown her. She'd told herself for so long that this was never going to happen, that this moment was impossible, that now she didn't have any idea how to handle it.

It took a moment for Mia to find her voice. "But I thought I couldn't get pregnant with my condition."

Dr. Misti-Cooper shrugged. "So did I, but apparently, you are a medical marvel. It's still very early, though, so we'll need to keep a close eye on both of you, but from what I can see now, you two look perfect."

The little dot shifted on the screen and Mia's heart filled with more love than she ever thought possible.

"You said it's a he?" she whispered, her eyes never leaving the screen.

"I call all these little guys 'he' until we know for sure," the doctor explained with a friendly chuckle. "It's still way too early to tell. The earliest we can find out is at ten weeks with a maternal blood test, but most people still find out at the twenty-week ultrasound."

"Twenty weeks?" Mia repeated. It felt like such a long time and yet absolutely not enough time at the same moment. She swallowed hard. Dr. Misti-Cooper gently patted her leg.

"You're going to have to take it easy. Be gentle with yourself. Given your history, I don't want you taking any unnecessary risks," the doctor told her. "No sports where you might fall. No horseback riding, ice-skating, bike riding, that kind of thing."

"Okay," Mia agreed. She wasn't going to do anything to risk this miracle baby. She was ready to sit in a padded room for the next nine months if it meant her baby would be safe.

The machine beeped as it finished printing out copies of the ultrasound picture.

"Here you go," the doctor said, handing her several copies. The image was just blurry black and white circles, but to Mia, it was the most beautiful thing she'd ever seen. "I'll go get you some information on what foods and medicines to avoid while you get dressed."

Mia nodded, not really paying attention to the doctor as she left. Mia was too busy staring at the picture in her hands. She was going to be a mother. There was a little person growing inside of her. She already felt incredibly protective of it.

"Don't worry little one," she whispered to the white dot in the photo "I've got you, and I'm not going to let anything happen to you. You're safe with me."

Chapter 30

 arter

CARTER SAT in the garage and went over the designs for his next year's car models and felt a wave of frustration wash over him. He wished he could just go to the plant and start on them now. There was so much that needed to be done that he couldn't do from his mountain home. As much as he loved being out on the ranch, it certainly made doing business ridiculously hard. He wished he could go down to the city for at least a couple of hours just so that he could get a few things accomplished.

Without access to his office and his usual business interactions, he felt out of control. He had far too much freedom out here, and he missed the hustle of the office. The ranch was great, but he craved the thrill of the deal and the excitement of being around people who shared his dream. He wasn't good at just sitting back and letting things happen, so being out here in the middle of nowhere was hard on him.

He sighed and pushed his chair away from the drafting table. If he was feeling like this, it meant it was time to take a break. He got up and went to the paddocks to see to his horses. This was the part that made being out here tolerable. He loved the horses and doing manual labor. It was so different from what he was paid to do that it was pleasurable.

The walk was chilly, but the sun still shone through the clouds, and the snows hadn't come yet. The mountain tops were white now, and frost covered the grass each morning, so it wouldn't be long now, but today was beautiful. A crisp, cool fall day with nothing to worry about. For the moment, the world was as it should be.

A security guard nodded respectfully as he passed and Carter returned the motion, almost like a salute. He hoped that whoever was sending the threats would be caught soon. He needed them to be caught so that he could go back to work and his real life.

Hopeful Dreamer nickered softly at him as he approached the fence to the big open space. The foal raised his head and began dancing around his mother with joy that his friend had come to visit him. If that wasn't enough to make him feel better, then nothing was, Carter thought to himself as he opened the gate and went inside the paddock.

It was amazing how much the little foal had grown in two months. He was still all legs and odd angles, but the grace of his sire was starting to show. He was a deep black with white forelegs and a star on his forehead. Star Dreamer was an appropriate name for him.

The foal nipped at his sleeve as he came close, asking him to play in the yellow grass. His mother watched, munching on a mouthful of grass stems. She knew that Carter would keep her baby safe, so she almost seemed happy to have someone else keep the energetic young foal entertained for a while.

Carter checked the colt over with his hands, making sure that he didn't have any burrs or injuries. He knew that Laura did this every evening when the horses came in, but it felt good to do it himself. If he was going to be stuck here, he might as well feel like he was useful.

Hopeful Dreamer's head popped up and she froze for a moment before deciding there was no reason for alarm and went back to eating. Carter followed her gaze to see Brian coming up to the fence. The big man had a smile on his face which made Carter hopeful for good news. He gave Star Dreamer one last pat before walking back to the fence. The colt tried to follow him until his mother scolded him for going too far.

"What's going on?" Carter asked as he got close. Brian stood away from the fence with his hands behind his back and looking like the professional he was.

"I have good news," Brian replied. "We have a lead. We got a hit on the fabric left on the porch bomb. The police are planning an arrest. We finally had enough information to put all the pieces together. This was the most frustrating puzzle I've ever worked on in my damn life."

"An arrest?" Carter asked. "They're that close?"

Brian nodded. "All signs point to a family member of the airbag death lawsuit. A father of one of the girls that died. We'd been looking into them, but nothing connected them until now. We know who it is now. His name is Fred Hillstone."

Carter stayed silent but nodded. He immediately recognized the name from the lists. His daughter was Beth and was nineteen when she died. He knew every name on the list of people that had died. He'd memorized them all. He could only imagine the amount of anger her father held toward him. He could understand it, but that didn't justify the death threats.

It made sense that it was someone from the airbag lawsuit. There were hundreds of people affected, many with deaths. The level of planning to get to him out here required true hate. Death could cause that. He had thought the fiasco with the airbags was behind him, but apparently, it wasn't. The settlement had been more than fair, but there wasn't a real way to put a price on a human life.

"The police are searching, but they haven't found him yet," Brian continued. "They believe he's fled to Wyoming, judging from his credit card purchases."

"It's almost over then, isn't it?" Carter asked, feeling his shoulders start to relax.

Brian nodded, and the smile came to his face. "Once he's in custody, you can go back to your regular life. You can go back to the city. You can go home to California."

The words didn't excite Carter like he thought they would. California suddenly seemed very far away from here. From Mia. From the kids. He would miss them all terribly. He found himself not wanting to leave after all.

He hadn't expected to fall for them like he did. They were the highlight of his days, and the idea that he would leave them behind was actually rather sad. The thought of saying goodbye to Mia made his heart tremble. She meant too much. Their conversations late at night cuddled together meant too much for him to just leave.

He loved her. He loved those kids.

The realization hit him like a punch to the gut. It wasn't lust or friendship. It was love. He loved those kids like they were his own, and he loved Mia even more. She completed him in a way that he never expected to find.

As much as he wanted to go back to his old life, his heart wanted to stay here too. He wanted both lives. Was it possible that he could have his life here and in California?

"Thank you for telling me, Brian," Carter said, putting a smile on his face. This was supposed to be good news. "Let me know when he's been apprehended."

Brian nodded and turned to continue patrolling the ranch. Carter watched him for a moment before turning around and going back to Star Dreamer and his mother. The colt whinnied and danced like it had been weeks instead of minutes since Carter left him. He was going to have to leave Star Dreamer too, he realized.

The little horse tucked his head under Carter's hand, positioning his head so that Carter would scratch the spot behind his ears that always seemed to be itchy. Carter chuckled and began scratching as the colt sighed with pleasure.

Carter stood in the meadow with his horses and stared at the horizon. He was trying to come up with a way that he could still be here and at his plant in California. Or maybe Mia could move? But the kids were in the system here. They couldn't go to California, and there was no way that Mia would leave them.

He sighed and shifted his feet. There had to be a way that he could have his old life with the people that he loved in his current one.

There had to be.

Chapter 31

Mia

"ARE YOU OKAY, MIA?" Grayson asked, tugging gently on Mia's hand as they walked to the barn for their Wednesday work session.

"Hmm? Oh, I'm fine," she replied, giving herself a shake and smiling down at him. Her thoughts had been on the baby growing in her stomach.

"Carter says that you can't let your thoughts wander when you're working with the horses," Grayson informed her. "You need to use your full brain."

Mia chuckled. "It's a good thing I'm not working with the horses today then, huh?"

On impulse, she knelt down and pulled the little boy into a hug. Grayson happily hugged her back. She took a deep breath in, pulling in his strawberry scented shampoo mixed with the sunshine in his hair. It smelled like innocence to her. He would never be this little again. Tears welled up in her eyes.

"You sure you're okay?" Grayson asked, pulling back. He frowned a little, and she realized she'd hugged him for a long time.

"I am," she promised. "Go catch up with your brother and sister. I need to go talk to Carter."

"Okay," he agreed before sprinting off down the path and into the barn.

Mia blinked back the sudden surprise tears and tried to gather herself. The hormones had her crying at everything it seemed like. It made what she was going to do today even harder. She knew she needed to tell Carter about the baby.

"I don't want kids." Carter's voice whispered through her mind. The conversation rippled through her head, telling her that this was a bad idea. He didn't want to be a father. He wouldn't want this life growing inside of her.

Tears threatened to fill her again. She wanted this life. And she knew she needed to tell him. It was the right thing to do.

Why tell him now? A voice in her mind whispered. *What if you miscarry? Why not wait until things are more certain?*

She sighed. She'd had this conversation with herself for the past twenty-four hours nonstop. She wasn't sure what was the right time to tell him was, but she knew that the sooner she did, the less she'd stress over it. Honesty was the best policy. That's what she told her kids, so she needed to be a good role model and do it herself.

Even if she was scared shitless. She needed to tell him.

Before she could back out or change her mind, she pulled out her phone to text him. But, just as she opened the message app, her phone buzzed with a message from him.

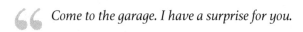

Come to the garage. I have a surprise for you.

THE SIMILARITY to what she was about to write made her chuckle. She was the one with a real surprise. She wondered what he wanted to show her since she was fairly certain he wasn't about to tell her he was pregnant.

She glanced to the barn to make sure all three kids were safe and with Laura. Grayson was giggling, and the other two wore big smiles that told her they were happy. They loved it here, and she hoped that they could continue to come even after the baby came.

Her lip was between her teeth as she thought about it. She wasn't sure what was going to happen in a little less than eight months. To be honest, she didn't want to think about it. She was going to have to take time off work, but these kids were her work. She wasn't sure how she was going to make sure they stayed together when she wasn't their social worker because she was on maternity leave.

She shook her head. That was a problem for another day. Today's problem was telling Carter. She could worry about the rest tomorrow.

The walk was somehow fast yet seemed to take forever. She knew it was just nerves. She was fairly sure that Carter would react well, but the possibility of him reacting negatively was what she was afraid of. What if he didn't think the child was his? What if he asked her to get rid of it? What if he never wanted to see her again? The what-ifs were the worst part.

She swallowed hard before knocking on the door and stepping inside. The garage was nice and warm, giving the place a cozy feel after the coolness outside. Carter stood from his desk, grinning from ear to ear as she came in.

"You said you have a surprise?" she asked. After he showed her his, she would tell him hers. Hopefully, he'd be in a good mood, and everything would go well.

He grinned and motioned to the side of the garage. There was a car covered by a white sheet that was new. She frowned slightly at it as he went over and pulled it off.

The vehicle underneath the sheet was a small SUV with shiny black paint. It took her a moment, but then she recognized it from the model and the designs he had shown her of the car he was designing.

"Is this what I think it is?" she asked, stepping forward to touch it. It was beautiful and sleek. She could barely believe it was real.

"What do you think?" Carter asked. He crossed his arms and then uncrossed them as he waited nervously for her opinion on the car.

"It's amazing," she whispered. "I didn't think it was ready yet."

"It's not," he admitted. "This is a prototype. I wanted to show it to you."

She looked over at him with wide eyes. "I get to see it?"

"You signed an NDA," he reminded her with a shrug. "Besides, I trust you."

He went to open the driver's side door, and she just stared at him. He trusted her. Just as he'd trusted she wouldn't get pregnant. Guilt nibbled on the edges of her mind.

"Carter," she started, needing to get this secret off her chest. But he didn't let her finish.

"Come here," he said, pulling her to the door. "I want to

show you how it turns on. I need your opinion on if there are enough cup holders, too."

She paused for a moment, trying to decide what to do.

Now isn't the right time, she told herself. She knew he wouldn't be able to focus on her right now, not with the car here. She wanted to have his full attention, and besides that, he was so happy and excited to show her the car. She didn't want to take this moment from him.

So she pushed her secret back down and smiled. "I'm sure I can always use more cup-holders."

Carter laughed and held the door open for her to get in. As she did, he ran around to the passenger side and got in.

"Here's the startup screen," he said. "The software is still being installed, so it's not as complete as it will be, but when it's done it will tell you how many miles of charge you have, the weather, traffic conditions, and it can sync to your calendar."

"Wow," Mia replied. The seat was insanely comfortable, and she loved the visibility of the car already. "This is incredible."

"You like it?" Carter asked. She loved that he wanted her opinion.

"Very much," she assured him. "I can't believe you brought it here."

He smiled. "There is just one more thing I need you to test out for me."

"What's that?" she asked. There were certainly enough cup holders, and everything looked like it was the perfect family vehicle.

"Come to the backseat," he said, opening up her door and helping her out. He opened the passenger door and helped her in. She slid easily along the leather backseat, and he followed her in.

"What am I testing for?" she asked, looking around. The backseat had a good amount of legroom and was comfortable, but it was exactly what she expected out of a backseat.

"This," he replied, catching her chin in his fingers and kissing her. He covered her mouth with his, slipping his tongue in at just the right moment to make her gasp. Desire filled her fast and strong. Her hand moved to tangle in his soft hair, wanting more of his kiss.

He chuckled, the sound low and sensual. With an easy grace, he twisted and reached for her leg, pulling her across his lap, so she straddled him. She pulled back, surprised with how easy the motion was.

"You've done this before, haven't you?" she asked, her voice light.

"What, made out in the backseat of a car?" He grinned. "Maybe once or twice. But never with a girl this pretty."

He reached up and stroked her cheek, making her smile.

"I'm sure you say that to all the girls," she murmured, leaning forward and kissing him.

He took a small kiss before shaking his head. "Nope, not all the girls. Just you."

Then he curled his hand around the back of her neck and drew her to him. Nothing could have stopped her from kissing him now. She moaned softly, swaying toward him, wanting much more than just a kiss.

She rocked her hips against him, feeling him harden beneath her. The idea that she could turn him on so completely with just a kiss and a hip rock made her feel powerful and sexy as hell. She rolled her hips again, loving how he rose to meet her and the low, lustful groan that escaped his perfect mouth.

"Do that again," he begged, his hands going to her hips.

She rolled her body, pressing her hips to his and watching his eyes dilate with pleasure. "Don't stop."

She kept rocking herself against the growing pressure in his jeans. It felt amazing, even through her pants. She was already thinking of ways to get them off.

She slid her hands under his shirt and slid them up along his muscular chest. She loved the strength she found there. He was firm and hard in all the right places as she coaxed his t-shirt up and over his head.

His arms were still in the t-shirt as it came up over his mouth. She held him there, arms tangled in the sleeves and blindfolded by his own clothing. He grinned with that sensual mouth of his, and she took the opportunity to kiss him.

He let her kiss him, gyrating his hips to the tempo of her kiss for a moment before freeing himself of the t-shirt. He tossed it on the seat next to him and looked up at her with those beautiful blue eyes that did her in every time.

With their eyes locked, he reached forward and undid the top button of her dress shirt. She didn't plan the low gasp of desire that escaped her, but she did love the way it made Carter grin. He undid another button.

She tipped her head back, closing her eyes and focusing on the sensation only to bump her head on the roof of the car.

"Ouch," she whispered, sitting back up and rubbing the back of her head. She chuckled and looked at the designer of the car. "There's something for you to fix."

"Raise the roof," he replied. "I'll put in on the list. I'm sure it will be a major selling point."

She chuckled, leaning forward to kiss him again. He felt so good against her body. Everything about him felt good. She let her body take control.

He undid another button, and she shivered with desire. She loved how he teased her. She loved everything about him.

He reached for the last button on her shirt when the knock came. Mia pressed her open shirt up against his chest as they both froze in their compromising position. The knock came again. Mia couldn't see who it was because they'd steamed up the windows.

"Mr. Williamson?" Brian's voice called out. "You asked me to notify you when the director of marketing was available. He's on the line."

Carter's made a bitter face. "So, of course, he's available *now*," he said quietly. He cleared his throat and raised his voice. "Thank you, Brian. Give me a second."

"I'm guessing it's important that you make this call," Mia said, still pressed up against him. She pulled back slightly to look at him better, making sure not to bump her head on the car ceiling.

Carter nodded. "It is. He was supposed to be busy for another hour."

"It's okay," Mia promised. She kissed his nose. "Take care of business, and I'll wait here."

He sighed. "This call is going to take a while. I probably won't be done until late tonight."

Mia thought for a moment, then smiled at him. "Take care of business," she said. "I'll still be here tomorrow. And I won't have the kids. No distractions."

He looked at her, and a slow smile filled his face. "Have I told you how amazing you are?"

She grinned and shrugged. "Just yesterday. But feel free to tell me again."

"You're amazing." His eyes danced across her face as if

he were taking her in and couldn't get enough of looking at her. "You are the best thing that's ever happened to me."

Mia's chest swelled, and her heart nearly burst with joy.

"You are the best thing that's ever happened to me, too," she whispered leaning forward and kissing him.

That's when the guilt hit. She should tell him, but she couldn't find the words. She shifted off of his lap, moving to the seat beside him as the kiss ended.

"Carter, there's something..." Her words faltered, and her courage to tell him failed him. Now wasn't the right time anyway.

"What?" Carter asked, his head popping out of the shirt as he put it back on.

"It can wait until tomorrow," she said, putting on a smile. "Go take your phone call."

He looked at her for a moment before nodding. "Okay. Thank you for understanding."

With a smile and a quick kiss on her cheek, he opened up the car door and stepped out. Brian was still standing off to the side with a phone in his hand. Carter took it and held it up to his ear, somehow transforming into the businessman in front of her eyes.

She slowly buttoned up her shirt and exited the car. Carter was at his drafting table, having an animated discussion. He turned when he heard the car door close, and he smiled at her. She nodded and waved before leaving the barn to go collect the kids.

Tomorrow, she decided. It had to be tomorrow.

Chapter 32

$\mathcal{M}$ia

MIA STOOD in front of the ranch house and took a deep breath. The smells of hay and clean mountain air filled her lungs, and she tried to steady herself. Today was the day. Today she was telling Carter.

The kids were at school, and she'd told her boss she was taking the rest of the day off, so there weren't any distractions. Today, she wasn't getting sidetracked by cars or kids or anything. Today, she was telling him that he was the father of her baby.

Just thinking the words made her heart stumble. She still wasn't sure how he was going to react, and that uncertainty gnawed at her. She loved him, and she was terrified that he might push her away because of this.

He didn't want children. He'd said it in interviews and even to her directly. She wanted him to be in her life, to be in their child's life, but she understood if he didn't want to be. This was something he had been very clear on not wanting. She wasn't sure how he was going to respond.

Mia glanced around the ranch. It seemed quieter without the kids here. She realized it wasn't just the lack of kids, but that security wasn't as present. There always seemed to be a uniformed presence haunting around the house and grounds, but today she couldn't see anyone.

She shrugged. It was odd, but she was kind of glad for it. The last thing she wanted was an audience for this. The security teams were usually very discrete, but this was between her and Carter.

Mia tipped her chin up and set her shoulders. This was happening. It was time.

She walked confidently up to the front door and opened it. She was expected, so she didn't feel the need to knock. The alarm system beeped twice as the door opened and once more when the door shut.

"Carter?" she called out. The house appeared empty.

"Upstairs," came the reply. Her heart did a somersault in her chest, and she had to try her best not to throw up. For a moment, she considered running back out to her car, but that would only delay the inevitable.

Mia paused for a moment at the bottom of the stairs, trying to center herself. She closed her eyes and tried to think positive thoughts. She wanted this baby, even if he didn't. She could do this.

It took more courage than she cared to admit to take the first step. Her hands shook on the wooden railing as she ascended. She walked past the big bedroom and down the hallway to the room he used as his study when he wasn't in the barn or the garage.

The room was masculine and warm. Leather furniture sat before a heavy wooden desk and books of all shapes and colors filled the walls. Carter sat at the desk working on his laptop, his head and shoulders framed by the big picture window behind him. The sunshine enveloped him like he was wearing a blanket. He looked so handsome sitting at his desk that she let herself just stare at him for a moment. He had on a long sleeved collared shirt today that looked good on him. It was pale blue, and it accented his eyes and showed off the broadness and strength of his shoulders.

Focus, she reminded herself as she wondered how the shirt would look on the floor. *No using sex to get out of it this time. Sex is how you got into this mess.*

"Mia," he greeted her warmly, looking up from his computer. "You look beautiful."

She blushed. She'd worn her favorite dress pants and her best button-up long sleeved shirt. She'd hoped that looking professional would give her more courage, but it didn't seem to be working. What she really wanted was a stiff drink, but that was definitely out of the question. The work outfit would have to do. "Thank you."

"You said you wanted to talk to me about something? Did you get more ideas for the car?"

Mia shook her head and took a tentative step into the office. Her palms were sweating. "No, but I do need to talk to you about something important."

He smiled and nodded. "Of course. Let me just finish this email, and we can talk. Have a seat; this will just take a second."

He motioned to one of the big leather seats in front of the desk and then quickly began typing. Mia sat gingerly on the edge of the seat. Her whole body was in knots. She placed her hands in her lap, fiddling with her nails. There was a rough edge on one, and she couldn't help but play with it while she waited.

"Okay," Carter announced. "I just hit send and--"

That was when the lights flickered, and the power went out. Downstairs, the alarm system chirped once before going silent. The usual hum of electricity through the house went dead.

"What kind of email did you send?" Mia teased.

"It wasn't that big," Carter replied with a frown, pushing a button on his computer.

"That's what she said," Mia chirped. Her nerves made her laugh a little too loud at her own joke.

Carter gave her a strange look for a second and checked his computer before trying to turn on a desk light. Nothing changed. With a frown, he picked up the landline telephone on his desk. For a moment, Mia chuckled that he had a landline. It made sense for him to have one since he used this for his business, but she had to get her nerves under control.

"It's dead," he said, hanging it up with a frown.

"Good thing for cell phones," Mia joked, pulling hers out. Except there was no signal. It was strange because she usually got good reception on her phone at the ranch. Her thoughts shifted away from what she was going to tell him to what was going on. "I don't have any bars."

"Me neither," Carter said, looking at his own phone.

A chill went through Mia. She rubbed her arms as Carter stood and looked out the window. She could see the tension mounting in his shoulders despite the easy way he moved. Something wasn't right, and they both knew it.

"There should be a security guard out there," he said quietly, peering out the window and frowning. The bright sunshine in the comfortable room felt strange. "Where is everyone?"

They were both silent and heard the front door open.

There was no beep of the security system, just the sweep and the whoosh before a wooden click. Mia held her breath, waiting for security to announce themselves. There was no sound. Mia and Carter's eyes met. His eyes went big for a moment before going firm and into business mode.

Carter held up his finger to his mouth. He hurried from the window and carefully closed the door to his office, being as careful as possible not to make a sound. Mia tried not to breathe. She was sure that Carter could hear the pounding of her heart.

He slid the lock into place on the door and stepped away back to his desk. Without saying a word, he held up his phone to the window, attempting to get service. The way his mouth thinned told her that it didn't work. She got up to join him and try her phone, even though she didn't hold out much hope.

Even next to the window, the reading on her phone didn't change. Carter went to his desk and pulled out a keypad and pressed a button. Nothing happened. Mia recognized the symbol on it as the same one as the security system. She figured it was an alarm trigger just for his office. He pressed it again. Nothing happened. There was no way to contact anyone. Their cell phones had no reception, the landline was down, and even the security system wasn't working.

"Did it work?" she whispered, coming closer to him. She felt safer the closer she was to him.

He shook his head. "No, but on the upside, security will be here in five minutes anyway."

"Really?" she asked, feeling just a little relief trickle through her. "How come?"

"If there's ever a power outage and signal stops coming in from the security system, security is to head directly to my last known location," he explained, his voice so quiet she could barely hear him. "So, they'll come here."

"That's good," she said with a small smile. He wrapped his arm around her and kissed her head.

"We'll be fine," he promised, giving her a squeeze. She leaned into him, glad that he was so confident.

The floorboards outside the office door creaked, and they both froze like rabbits. Mia had never held so still in her life, and she was sure that Carter had stopped breathing he was so statue-like.

"I know you're in there, Carter."

The voice was male and deep. Mia didn't recognize it, and from the way Carter tensed, he didn't recognize it either. There was an angry quality to the voice that made her blood run cold. The tone promised violence.

"You killed my daughter. Now, I'm going to kill you."

Chapter 33

$\mathcal{M}$ia

"YOU KILLED MY DAUGHTER. Now, I'm going to kill you."

The words were even and calm, yet so full of hatred that Mia winced. The man on the other side of the door wasn't nervous or afraid. He was calm and ready to deal out the justice he felt the world deserved. A justice with Carter dead.

The man started to pound on the door. It shook from every blow and Mia didn't know how long it would hold. It was a heavier door than she was used to, but the man outside was determined, and a little bit of wood and metal wasn't about to stop him. This had to be the man sending death-threats to Carter. He had to have found a way to turn off the security system and phones. She wondered how he'd gotten security to leave.

It didn't matter, though. He was here now. He was here and ready to carry out his threats.

Carter didn't hesitate. He went to the window, ready with a plan. He grunted with the effort of lifting the big window open. Once it was open, he pushed on the screen, letting it tumble to the ground. He poked his head out and motioned to her.

"We can jump from here," he said, pointing down. Mia realized that Laura hadn't gotten all the hay put away as some was below the window. "The hay will break the fall, and it's only one story. We'll be fine."

Mia was suddenly glad that Laura was so busy that she hadn't finished that chore yet. She looked out the window and stopped. She couldn't jump. Even just one story into a pile of hay.

"I can't," she whispered.

"Yes, you can," Carter told her with a gentle smile. "I'll be right here with you."

The door shook, and a fragment of wood flew off it as a gunshot sounded. They both ducked, turning in time to watch a fragment of the door hit the floor. The door had stopped the bullet, but barely. The man outside was getting angrier now that the door hadn't given way.

"You killed her," the intruder wailed, losing his calm as he slammed his body into the door again so hard the whole room shook.

"I can't jump," Mia repeated, stepping away from the window.

"I'll hold your hand," Carter coaxed, still smiling like he had all the time in the world. He held out his hand to her. "It'll be fine. I promise."

Mia shook her head, and she let out a terrified gasp. "I can't jump. I'm pregnant."

The words hit Carter like a slap. He stared at her, then down to her stomach, then back up to her face. The color drained from his cheeks. He hadn't been afraid of the intruder, but he was afraid of her words.

"YOU KILLED HER," the man wailed, sending another piece of wood from the door flying. It would only take a few more hits, and he would be through. Mia held no illusions as to the fact that she was dead as soon as that happened. The death-threat sender knew she was important to Carter. She was just glad the kids were at school and safe there.

Carter ran around to the opposite side of the desk and tossed the leather chairs to the side as if they were made of plastic. He hopped back over the desk, and braced his shoulder against the heavy wood and pushed. It didn't move.

Mia hurried to his side and put her hands on the heavy desk to help.

"No," he told her gruffly, pushing her hands off of it. He took a breath and braced his shoulder again. The seam on his shoulder ripped as his muscles tensed and he used every ounce of strength he had to push the desk.

The desk had to weigh a ton, but he moved it up against the door. He was shaking when he finished.

"YOU CAN'T STOP ME," the voice cried. Anger and pain filled the words as he slammed into the door again. The door shook, but this time the desk held it in place. It wouldn't last forever though. All the man needed to do was keep hitting above the desk, and he would be inside.

Carter grabbed her hand, pulling her to the closet. He threw it open.

"Get inside," he commanded. His voice was low and dangerous. "You should be safe. He doesn't want you. He doesn't know you're here."

She moved inside the closet.

"I'll stay out here. Whatever you hear, don't make a

sound." His mouth was thin, and she couldn't look away from the rip on his shirt. She reached for his hands.

"Carter..." She looked up at him, knowing he was protecting her. There was so much that she needed to say. There was so much that she still needed to tell him, that he needed to know. This wasn't the place. "I didn't want to tell you like this."

The door shook and the man outside screamed and tried again.

"When did you find out?" Carter asked quietly. His eyes stayed on their hands, not wanting to look into her eyes. At least he hadn't pulled away yet.

"A couple of days ago." Her voice caught at the end.

"A couple of days?" Anger flashed through his blue eyes and Mia shrunk down as he took his hands away.

"I didn't know how to tell you," she whispered. "I'm sorry. I'm so sorry for all of this."

A rage scream filled the air, and the door shook again. Another bullet hit the door, making a large, strange dent in the fortified wood. "YOU KILLED HER. YOU DESERVE TO DIE."

Carter's shoulders slumped. He raised his eyes from her hands to her face. There was such grief and betrayal that it broke her heart. She felt a tear run down her cheek, but she didn't move. She didn't know what to do or what to say. She turned her face from his gaze, her heart already shattering.

There was a blast from outside the door, and Mia was sure it was the end. She was sure that the man had finally broken down the solid wood door and was going to kill them all. He was going to kill Carter, her and their baby.

But the door remained intact. There were shouts and a scream from the other side. Mia held her breath until the shouting stopped. It felt like ages.

"Mr. Williamson? You can come out now." The voice this time on the other side of the door was Brian. Mia recognized it and sagged with relief. She felt like her knees were going to give out.

Carter stepped away from her and went to the door. He unlocked it.

"I have the desk next to the door. Tell me when to push," he told Brian.

At Brian's signal, Carter used his feet against the wall and his back to the desk to help push while the security team on the other side pushed as well. The floor made a horrible noise as the desk scraped against it, but they were free.

"Are you all right, sir?" Brian asked, poking his head through the doorway. "The threat has been removed."

Mia came out of the closet, surprised that her feet were steady enough to walk. Through the open window, she could see security vans arriving, and the howl of police sirens floated through the air. She noticed how cold it was in the room with the window wide open.

"I'm fine," Carter told him, pushing past and through the open door. "I just need some air."

Mia stared after him. He was angry. He had every right to be.

"Are you all right, ma'am?" Brian asked her, coming into the room.

She nodded meekly. Physically she was fine, but she wasn't sure how she was emotionally just yet.

"Excuse me," she said, knowing that she needed to go after Carter. She needed to talk to him. So she went through the broken door and hurried after the man she loved.

Chapter 34

M ia

MIA GLANCED at the office door on her way out and recoiled. It was a miracle the man hadn't gotten through. Just a few more moments and he would have had them. The door on the opposite side of the office was in tatters and stamped with blood. She could only assume it was the man's with his attempts to get in.

She wasn't far behind Carter. She could see the blue of his shirt as he disappeared out the front door. A sea of uniformed security stood in her way, but she wiggled between them hot on his tail. She had to catch him.

Outside, the police had finally arrived. Ten squad cars all stood in the big driveway loop of the ranch with more lining up down the road. It hurt her eyes to look at all the lights, but she did see an officer putting a man into the back of one.

He was tall and relatively good looking. He had the dark

uniform of the security team, though it didn't seem to fit him very well. The man looked up, and she saw his eyes. They were ice cold and full of such fury that she had to take a step back even though she wasn't close to him.

"He killed her," the man screamed, starting to thrash. Spit sprayed from his mouth like venom as he tried to get away.

She took another step back, needing to get away from him. The police had him, but given her afternoon, she wouldn't feel safe until he was firmly behind bars. Her back pressed up against another body, and she spun.

Brian held up his hands to show he wasn't trying to startle her. To be fair, she had backed into him.

"How did he get on the property?" Mia asked crossing her arms. Anger flared in her belly. It was supposed to be Brian's job to keep Carter safe. "Where did he get that uniform? Is he one of yours?"

"No ma'am," Brian assured her. "The man stole Ben's uniform."

He pointed to the side of the house where an ambulance sat hidden among the sea of police cars. Sitting in the opened back was Ben wearing a blood-stained t-shirt and jeans. He had an ice-pack to his head and was trying to answer the paramedic's questions. Even from this distance, he looked dazed.

"What happened to him?" Mia asked, momentarily losing her anger. Ben was a good guy.

"We found Ben tied up in the backseat of his truck," Brian explained. "Our perp is his landlord. He's been using Ben's ID badge to get on and off the property. He was able to know Ben's schedule, and thus get access to the security schedule. That's why we couldn't catch him."

"Is Ben going to be okay?" Mia watched as a paramedic shone a light into Ben's eyes.

"Hillstone hit him hard enough to knock him out. Cut his head open in the process. Ben will be out of commission for a while, but I think he'll be okay." Brian shook his head. "Hillstone thought this was his last chance at getting Mr. Williamson, so he didn't hold back."

Mia swallowed hard and looked away from Ben. If Hillstone was willing to put an innocent man in the hospital with a concussion and stitches, there was no doubt he would have killed them both. It made her stomach twist, and she felt nauseous. Her hands went protectively to the small life growing in her belly.

Carter... she needed to find him. She glanced around and saw him walk into his garage. She took a deep breath. She knew he probably wanted to be alone right now, but she needed to talk to him. He needed to hear that this wasn't the end of the world.

She thanked Brian and headed toward the garage. The door was cracked open, telling her that he was expecting her to follow. If he didn't want visitors, he would have closed and locked the door. She took it as a good sign and knocked twice before pushing it open and stepping inside.

Carter sat with his back to her, busy drawing something on his drafting table. The sound of his pen on the screen filled the space between them. He didn't look up at her as he worked.

She walked over slowly, chewing on her bottom lip so hard she was sure she was going to draw blood soon. Her footsteps stopped as she stood off to his left. He was sketching out a new car.

"Carter, I want to explain," she said softly into the silence. Her hands twisted against one another and that twisted stomach feeling was back. She looked around, noting where the trash bins were just in case her lunch came up.

"How did this happen?" he asked, his voice gruff. The pen flowed across the screen, giving shape to a sleek, fast-looking car.

"Well, I believe it happened in Vegas," she replied.

His hand paused above the drawing, and he turned to study her. There was a wild gleam in his eye that she wasn't sure of. It looked dangerous as he evaluated her.

"I didn't mean for this to happen," she said quickly. Her emotions were coming up again and it was only seconds before she knew she was going to burst into tears and start sobbing. The adrenaline of what just happened still pumped through her, but she had to get this out before she broke down. "The doctors said I would never get pregnant. That it was impossible. I'm so sorry. I know this isn't what you wanted. I'm so, so sorry."

It was all just too much. The adrenaline, the danger, the hurt, the fear, the sorrow, and the shock. Her knees buckled, and she sagged to the floor. Once her knees were down, full body sobs racked her entire frame. Every inch of her cried. It was ugly and raw, but she couldn't hold it back anymore.

Suddenly, his arms were around her, and her face pressed into his strong shoulder. He held her tightly to him as she sobbed. Tears streamed down her face, and her nose ran, but he held her tight. He didn't let her go. He just held her to him, rubbing her back and making quiet, soothing noises as he let her release the torrent of emotions inside of her.

"I'm so sorry," she whispered once the crying became more manageable. She hadn't cried like that since she was a child, though to be fair, she'd never had her and her child's life threatened before either.

Carter took her chin between his thumb and forefinger, raising her face to look at him. His blue eyes were like the sea after a storm. She didn't see anger there anymore.

"Don't be," he told her.

"But you don't want kids," she replied. She wiped her nose on the back of her hand and sniffled.

"You're right. I didn't," he agreed with a small nod. He smiled gently. "Until I met you. And Alexander, Lily, and Grayson. Now I want everything. Now I want it all."

Mia's heart stalled. She was going to start crying again but for an entirely different reason this time. He caressed her cheek and smiled as she looked her over.

"I love you, Mia," he told her, kissing her forehead. He met her eyes and smiled. She could see excitement forming in their deep blue pools. "And I will love our child."

Chapter 35

ia

"Mia, where are you?" Grayson asked over the phone. "You were supposed to be here ten minutes ago."

Mia put on her turn signal and worked her way to the edge of the highway so she could get off and head up to the ranch.

"I'm really sorry, Grayson," Mia replied, checking her mirrors. "The traffic today is terrible. The snow is just slowing everything down."

"How long until you get here?" the little boy asked, obviously pouting.

Mia raised her eyebrows at the phone. Grayson usually didn't care when she got to the ranch. In fact, the later she was, the happier he was because it meant more time in the barn with Star Dancer. He loved that little colt.

"Five minutes, tops," she promised, stepping on the gas and zooming up to the dirt road leading to the ranch.

"Okay!" Grayson replied cheerfully and he ended the call. Mia shook her head and kept driving. Everyone seemed to be behaving oddly today.

First, Laura had asked the kids to come work at the ranch today, even though it wasn't their usual day. She said there was something important that she needed them to work on, but she was tight lipped about any other information. When Mia called Margie to let her know, Margie wasn't surprised. In fact, she seemed to already know about it.

Then, her boss had been strange all day. She had come and taken the kids' paperwork a couple of days before for an audit but was refusing to give it back. Mia had no idea what that was about.

Now, on her way back from work, Grayson was calling about her being late. Mia tried to think if there were any birthdays or anniversaries that she was forgetting about. She couldn't think of anything. There was no good reason for everyone to be acting so strangely.

"Must be a full moon tonight," Mia murmured, pulling up to the ranch. "Everyone's just turning into werewolves. Or maybe they were all abducted by aliens and I'm the only human left."

She chuckled as she pulled into the ranch. It was probably just her and her hormones. Being pregnant was doing strange things to her body. She'd never known until now just how much her state of mind depended on her hormonal balance.

As she came to a stop in front of the ranch, the front door opened and Grayson ran out. He raced to the side of the car with a huge grin on his face. He didn't have a jacket or coat on, and the white snow stood out against his dark hair.

"What are you doing out here?" Mia asked, getting out of the car. "Where's your coat?"

Grayson shrugged and took her hand, pulling her back to the house. "Come with me."

The little boy practically vibrated with excitement. Mia wondered what in the world had him in such a state. Alexander was waiting by the door, hopping up and down as they came in.

"She's here!" Alexander yelled into the house as Mia took off her coat and set her bag down. She had to hurry because both boys grabbed her hands and pulled her down the stairs to the basement.

Carter and Lily were waiting in the common room, both with grins to match the boys. Mia was sure something was up. They had some sort of surprise for her. Her hands went to her belly. Did they know?

"What's going on?" Mia asked as Grayson and Alexander released her hands and went to stand next to Carter and Lily.

"We've been adopted," Lily announced. Her whole face lit up with a smile as she said the words.

"What?" Mia felt the wind go out of her. No one had told her they'd been adopted. These kids were special to her. They couldn't just go to anyone! No wonder her boss had stolen their files! "Who adopted you?"

Carter stepped forward with a guilty smile. "I did."

The anger of her children being sent to a stranger went out like a candle. She needed to sit down.

"What? How?" Questions swirled around in her mind, never combining to form complete sentences. Instead, she just went to the couch and sat down hard.

"Your boss and I are getting to be very good friends,"

Carter replied. He sat next to her, taking her hand in his and smiling.

"You adopted them?" Joy started to warm in her heart and spread through her chest and out to her fingers and toes. If she couldn't adopt them, then Carter was the only other person in the world she was okay with them being with. She pushed away the small hurt that they would be his and not hers. That wasn't important.

"Yes," Carter replied. He glanced at the kids who all nodded vigorously. He then took a deep breath, cleared his throat, slid off the couch and got down on one knee in front of her. "Would you join us? We're not a family without you."

Mia stared at him as he reached into his back pocket and pulled out a black velvet box. He flipped it open and held it out to her. Inside was the most beautiful diamond ring she'd ever seen.

"Mia Amesworth, will you marry me and make me the happiest man in the world?" Carter asked, holding out the box.

She looked at her kids, all three with smiles as big as their faces and nodding away, then to Carter. His blue eyes held such love and warmth. There was just enough nervousness to make her love him even more.

"Yes," Mia whispered. "Yes, yes, YES!"

She threw her arms around his neck, the yes's coming in quick succession. She couldn't stop saying yes. He wrapped his arms around her and laughed, kissing her tear covered cheeks. The kids rushed over, joining in on the hug and laughing along with them.

There were hugs and kisses all around. Each child got their own hug, then took turns hugging one another. Mia's heart beat with pure joy. She no longer had blood in her veins, she had happiness. She didn't need oxygen anymore ld have done if I had said no?" Mia asked Carter once everyone had settled down and all the hugs were out of their systems.

Carter looked over at the kids. "Do you think they would have let me return them?"

"Hey!" Alexander shouted, but Carter pulled him into a hug and ruffled his hair. It was obvious to all that he wasn't going to let these kids out of his life.

"Just kidding. I promised you guys a forever family, and I wouldn't dream of going back on that," Carter promised. Lily and Grayson laughed. He looked at Mia and frowned slightly. "Were you thinking of saying no?"

Mia kissed his cheek. "Not in a million years," she replied. "It was just such a big gesture, I was curious."

Carter leaned over and kissed her. The kids made grossed out noises, but none of them lost their smiles.

"Since it's a day for big news..." Carter said slowly. His eyes went to Mia's belly and then back to her face.

Mia thought for a moment, then nodded. "They deserve to know what they're getting in to."

Carter nodded. "Kids, we have another announcement to make about our family."

Alexander and Grayson frowned. Lily's eyes went wide as she figured it out.

"I'm pregnant," Mia stated. "We're due in April."

Lily screamed and hugged her. "I'm so excited! I hope it's a girl!"

"I don't get it," Grayson said. "You have homework due in April?"

Carter smiled. "Not homework. A baby. Mia's going to have a baby in April. My baby."

Grayson thought about it for a moment before a slow smile filled his small face. "I get to be a big brother." He looked more pleased than a cat with cream.

Alexander frowned. "Do I have to share a room?" he asked. He motioned to the basement. "There's no room for a nursery here."

"No, you don't have to share a room," Carter promised with a chuckle. Alexander gave a relieved sigh.

"Then it's awesome," Alexander announced, his smile quickly returning.

"Actually, that's something I wanted to ask you guys." Carter looked around at his large family. "Do you want to live here, or in California?"

"California?" Lily repeated. She grew pensive. "Why not here?"

"My business is centered in California," Carter explained. "If you don't want to move, it's okay. I want my family to be happy."

"I just got friends here," Alexander said. He shrugged but didn't look excited.

Carter looked around and then smiled. "Then I'll just have to move my business here."

"You can do that?" Mia asked.

"I told you, I'm not the CEO anymore. I don't manage anyone. I'm just an outside consultant. I can do whatever I want," Carter replied. "And what I want, is all of you."

Mia watched as Carter looked around at each face. Mia, Lily, Alexander, Grayson, and even at Mia's stomach for the future face to come. They were a family. This is what love looked like. This is what a forever kind of love looked like.

ABOUT THE AUTHOR

New York Times and USA Today Bestseller Krista Lakes is a thirtysomething who recently rediscovered her passion for writing. She is living happily ever after with her Prince Charming. Her first kid just started preschool and she is happy to welcome her second child into her life, continuing her "Happily Ever After"!

Thank you for supporting an indie author. Anything you can do, whether it be writing a review, or even simply telling a fellow reader that you enjoyed this, helps me out immensely. Thanks!

Krista would love to hear from you! Please contact her at Krista.Lakes@gmail.com or friend her on Facebook!

Further reading:

Made in the USA
San Bernardino, CA
22 July 2017